Wilberforce Lega

The inspector passed his reluctant hand over the death mask; a true mask, he reassured himself, as he discovered no openings in that grim countenance. His hands moved mechanically as his spirit revived. He found the fastening at the back of the mask, hidden in the hair; he pulled off the old man's false head and face to disclose another, more in keeping with the body, quite surely attached to it, pale, with lips drawn back from gleaming teeth, dead but real.

Mr. Mancini was staring at the mask in the inspector's hand.

"It is Mr. Wilberforce," he gasped. "It is a perfect likeness. I never saw it in his room. I never knew—"

"Never mind about your Mr. Wilberforce," said Inspector Vincent roughly. "This man. Have you ever seen him before?"

"No," answered Mancini, who had turned his back on the corpse.

The two ambulance men, being used to strange unpleasant sights, had been only mildly shocked by the nasty joke played on this drowned young man. They were now covering him with the sheet they held, but stopped at an order from Vincent.

"But you know him?" he said to Jim, who had scrambled up from his knees, his face working with relief, bewilderment and a mounting joy. "You're sure. I can see it. Look again."

Jim looked and swallowed and turned away.

Other titles in the Walker British Mystery Series

JOSEPHINE
BELL
The Wilberforce Legacy

WALKER AND COMPANY · NEW YORK

First published in the United States of America in 1969 by the
Walker Publishing Company, Inc.

This paperback edition first published in 1984.

ISBN: 0-8027-3096-5

Library of Congress Catalog Card Number: 69-15714

Printed in the United States of America

10 9 8 7 6 5 4 3 2 1

CHAPTER ONE

The Gardenia Lodge Hotel lay silent under the hot midday Caribbean sun. Nothing moved in the parched untidy drive that curved up from the busy road outside between banks down which sprawled overgrown withering grass. Near the entrance to this drive a tilted notice board declared the property to be FOR SALE. In the apparent desertion of the place at this hour, its sad neglect, its seemingly placid acceptance of decay, it might, if anyone had been interested, have turned the notice into an urgent call for help, a last appeal, even a cry of despair.

But no one was interested. Passers-by were used to the flaking paint on the pillars at the entrance to the drive. They no longer read the for sale notice, streaked with grime, leaning over as if exhausted by its long vigil, its total failure. Like many such hotels or guest houses, formerly busy with the visiting friends and relations from England of the administrators of this island of San Fernando, it was in process of being swallowed up by the surrounding commercial development and the steady decline, since independence, of its former purpose.

At the upper end the drive opened into a wider space, on the one side the open door of an office, on the other a shaded verandah leading into a dark corridor.

The general air of desertion was not relieved, but rather intensified by the presence of a thin black cat moving slowly back and forth between the two open entrances. There seemed to be no purpose in its movement. It paid no attention to the lizards that shot across the gravel under its nose, some to dart into the bushes below the verandah, some to run effortlessly up the dirt-streaked walls, to cling there, with all four legs spread sideways, suddenly motionless, tail not even twitching, perhaps intent upon an unseen prey, perhaps in fear of attack, perhaps simply to recover from its recent activity.

A small car turned into the drive and rushed up it from the main road, roaring in low gear. Even this sudden noise brought no sign of life from the one-storey hotel buildings, neither from the office nor from the owner's verandah opposite, nor the visitors' verandah at the end of the wide space, not even from the kitchens, tucked away behind the bushes and dust bins.

The car stopped with a jerk and a last misplaced roar from the engine. The postman in it jumped out and disappeared into the office. He stood there for a second, recovering his sight from the glare outside. He was not wearing sunglasses. His uniform cap was pushed back on tight-curled hair, his very black face ran with sweat. His official uniform was not designed for midday wear; in any case was quite unsuited to the tropics, being made of stout cloth and fastening to the neck, though the man wore it open down the front over a gleaming white shirt.

When he had wiped the sweat from his eyes and recovered his sight, he addressed a girl seated behind a wide counter with a small telephone exchange beside her. She had not moved at all when he came in. She did not move now, only looked at him, her smooth pale-brown face attentive, her large dark-brown eyes grave.

"Telegram," he said, holding out the yellow envelope. "Same again. This man Wilber—Wilber—"

"Wilberforce," she said, taking the envelope. "What so special in this name, man?"

"But only this morning. A letter, wasn't it? Then telegram— Now this. Telegram again, miss."

The girl shrugged, putting the yellow envelope down on the counter as if she preferred not to hold it.

"Is a telegram, you know," the postman protested. "Not just letter. Maybe an answer—"

"He always sleeps, afternoon," the girl said, quietly. "No good to wake him. Sleeps very deep."

It was the postman's turn to shrug. He moved away from

the counter back to the drive. The girl sat without moving, staring at the telegram. But when the sound of the post office car had passed out of hearing, merging with the unending but distant noise of traffic in the main road, she got up slowly and walked through the burning heat outside to the darkness of the corridor opposite.

At the first door in it she paused, hesitated, stooped to the keyhole, found it blocked by the key on the inside and stood up again, uncertain. In the deep shade of the corridor her emerald green, tightly fitting dress lost its brilliance and its hard outline. Her pale-brown face in shadow was darker than it appeared under the sun. The yellow envelope in her hand stood out sharply against the shadowed dress.

Baulked of her first attempt to see into the room the girl took hold of the handle of the door to turn it noiselessly, push the door open an inch or two and peer in. The bed, she knew, lay under the window and the window gave on to the verandah. So, from the tiny crack of the opening she had made she could see, in the close-curtained, darkened room, where the old-fashioned air conditioner buzzed faintly, the dim shape of the bed, the sheeted unmoving figure on it, the pale face on the pillow.

A man moved slowly down the corridor from the darkened lounge at its far end. The lounge curtains had been kept drawn since the television was installed, two years before. Against this added darkness the man was visible only as a white vest or singlet, moving slowly towards the girl. Black face and arms, black trousers, black feet in black soft slippers, slowly defined themselves as he came closer. When he reached her he stopped, moved his long thin body sideways to the support of the wall, at the same time taking the door handle from her grasp to close the door very softly.

"Wot you got there, Paula?" he asked, in a low murmur. "Same ting again? Mas'r Wilb again?"

She nodded solemnly, then thrust the yellow envelope towards him.

"You take it, Jim. He's friend to you. You're not afeared."

"Why should I be feared? Mas'r Wilb just a poor old man. So very old—he not here with us all the time."

The girl shivered, backing away from the old white man's door, which she now saw was again opening very slowly, though she had not seen or heard the handle turn. She always wanted to run when Mr Wilberforce appeared. A moment ago he had been stretched on his bed, asleep. Now—

She had time, before the door was fully open, to thrust the telegram into Jim's hand and leap away, out on to the verandah, down a step to the drive, up a step into the office, a flash of bright green in the sun, two pale-brown shapely legs, two smart white sling-back sandals, in swift, elegant motion.

Jim could not help watching the legs. His wife had had legs like that when he married her, he thought with amusement, seeing her as he had left her in the kitchen a minute ago, short flowered dress halfway up her stout thighs as she leaned forward over the pots and pans simmering spicily on her oil stoves. Fifteen years and six babies had done this to Therese, his wife. Or was it her French blood? She had been born in Guadalupe, where many people had French blood.

Why was Paula so upset? Why did she always begin to shiver when she saw Mas'r Wilb? *Saw!* He whipped round, the telegram held out stiffly at arm's length, because he too had failed to hear the door open, but he knew as he was in the act of turning that the old man had come out.

Not right out. He was, in fact, still in his room, in the doorway, holding on to the posts at either side. He said, in his usual, almost inaudible whisper, "That for me, Jim?" meaning the telegram, which was just in front of his face, shaking a little as Jim's arm shook.

"Yes, sah. Foe you, sah." As Mr Wilberforce still kept his hands on the doorposts, leaning out between them, his pale face and pale eyes quite motionless, Jim repeated desperately, "For you, Mas'r Wilb. Paula took it. Postman come in van, one, two minutes. Gone now, sah."

"I heard the van," Mr Wilberforce whispered.

He stood up, took his hands from the doorway, and accepted the telegram, but without looking at it.

"My tea on the verandah, Jim, in five minutes from now," he said.

"Very good, sah," answered Jim, briskly. He turned to walk, almost run, up the corridor and through the empty lounge into the empty dining room and from there into the hotel kitchen, where Therese was still occupied with her preparations for the dinner that evening. He told her about the telegram, the second that day. He repeated Mr Wilberforce's order for tea.

"He ate no lunch," Therese declared. "I give him sandwich. You go dress yourself, man. Ought to be ashamed Mas'r Wilb see you naked."

They both laughed widely, teeth gleaming. But Jim went off obediently to get into a white shirt and jacket, fit now to serve tea on a tray to Mas'r Wilb in his usual wicker armchair on the other, the long verandah, outside the darkened lounge.

When he got there with the tea, the old man had not yet arrived. Jim put down the tray on a wicker table, took a few steps back to the open door of the lounge and looked up the corridor. No one there. He went back on to the verandah to guard the sandwiches against possible marauders in the shape of half-starved cats, inquisitive stray dogs and even wandering children, hunting for profit of any kind in remote, unguarded spots such as the Gardenia Lodge Hotel.

Jim leaned against one of the pillars supporting the verandah roof. The drive beyond the small ill-kept lawn was screened from the verandah by a row of bougainvillaea bushes, their heavy drooping clusters of scarlet, crimson, pink or yellow flowers filling the gaps between the branches. Perhaps it was the verandah that was screened from the drive. It must have been so in the old days when visitors in cars, or earlier in pony carriages, drove in and out continually. Jim was not thinking of those earlier days, though he had already begun work in the place then as a kitchen boy. He was thinking about the old man who had lived there for over a year and had had not a single letter, not even a postcard, until this day. *A letter and two telegrams!*

His thoughts broke off abruptly as he heard the familiar shuffling sound behind him. He spun round, bent to the table where the tray rested and moved it a little to allow Mr Wilberforce to drop awkwardly into the wicker armchair behind it.

"Thank you," the old man said in his usual hoarse whisper.

He moved forward to inspect his sandwiches. Jim whipped the cover off them with one hand while picking up the teapot with the other. He poured tea with a flourish, almost filling the cup, then stopping, the teapot held in mid air.

"Thank you," Mr Wilberforce repeated, carrying through the usual ritual. "I will pour the milk myself."

Jim murmured, as usual, "Very good, sah," and retreated to the kitchen, where he expressed his bewildered disappointment to his wife.

"Jus same's every day," he complained. "Might never no letter no telegram come for him. From England, too."

"That was cable then, man," Therese corrected. "You ignorant not know long way telegram is cable."

"It was letter from England. Telegrams perhaps from here in San Fernando. Ask Paula."

Mr Wilberforce, eating his excellent sandwiches without much appetite, had no doubts about the provenance of his three pieces of communication and liked them no better for it. When he found himself alone he took the two telegrams and the letter from his pocket and read them all again, in the order in which they had arrived.

The letter had come by the morning post. It was from his sister, Lucy Maclean, a widow for three years now. After some perfunctory remarks about her own health and circumstances, not affluent—since Alec Maclean had been only fifty-eight when he died—but comfortable enough, she thanked God, she went on to express anxiety on her brother's account. She had always understood, she wrote, the reasons for Ben continuing to live abroad, though George had been dead nearly ten years and she was sure no one remembered his case. His former partners were all dead or retired, 'that woman' had made one attempt to see her but gave up when she refused, absolutely, to have anything to do with her.

Mr Wilberforce took his eyes from the letter at this point, removing his pale gaze to the bougainvillaeas, comparing their generous abundance and vivid colour with his memory of brother George's beautiful, unfortunate mistress, remembering how he himself had saved her from the worst consequences of George's final disaster. With no personal profit, he remembered wryly. Had she wanted to console Lucy, he wondered, or be herself consoled? Well, Lucy had refused to see her so he would never know. The ghost had risen momentarily in this letter and had sunk again without trace—without troubling him either, he noted with faint satisfaction.

He picked up the letter again. Young George was giving trouble. It was evident that Lucy would have denied the young man, too, if she had dared. But she did not dare. Young George wanted his uncle's address. By bullying her, even to the point of blackmail, she had been forced to send it to him. Perhaps it was natural he should want to see his uncle. He might be, he must be, crazy to think what he did, but he was George's son.

Again Mr Wilberforce paused in his reading, first to pour himself out some more tea, secondly to consider what Lucy had said. The old, old suspicion. He smiled at this thought, the grin displacing the deepcut lines round his mouth for a fleeting second. Lucy herself too, perhaps. No, she didn't understand, had never been told, the whole story of George's downfall. Nor the ultimate results. The real point of the letter, far more important than the vague news of young George, lay on the last page.

"Alison very much wants to see you again," Lucy wrote.

"She has never forgotten the kind, tall, handsome uncle who gave her such wonderful presents on her birthdays. She has just taken her degree in English with a first and is wondering what sort of job to go for. She is not very keen on teaching. So I have suggested she goes out to San Fernando for a few weeks, as a holiday and to see you. She has booked her passage quite cheaply on a merchant ship that takes a few passengers. Actually she is now on her way out. The ship is called *Benito*. She means to book a room at your hotel. Perhaps she wanted it to be a complete surprise but I consider it only fair to you to warn you of her arrival. That is why I am sending this to you direct by air mail and not to that solicitor of yours. I have never understood why you should be so cagey about your whereabouts. Also I wanted to tell you direct, not through Mr Gopal, about young George, in case he tries to get in touch and upset you—"

She ended with affectionate wishes that were entirely conventional and without meaning or sincerity, Mr Wilberforce decided, finishing his tea. The girl was another matter and George, his nephew, a thorough damned nuisance. Two telegrams from George. Both on the same day, both announcing his imminent arrival. Why two? Why come to San Fernando at all?

He pushed away the table and stood up, waiting for his stiff knees to unbend. There were two things Paula in the office could do for him. The first was to tell him if a Miss Alison Maclean had booked a room at the hotel and the second was to discover the date when the *Benito* was expected to dock at the island.

Paula raised her finely marked black eyebrows when she saw Mr Wilberforce, after a painful ascent of the step from the drive, shuffle into her office. She put down the newspaper she was reading and waited.

He was a sad wreck of a man, she thought, pitying him, no longer scared as she had been when he opened his door behind her so softly in the fierce heat of the afternoon. So softly, so unexpectedly, so very soon after she had seen him fast asleep. Or only pretending to sleep. Then why?

Now, with the shadows lengthening in the drive, he was an object of pity, not fear. His face was so pale, so lined, his hair pale, too, not the cheerful, positive white of age, but grey, light grey, the same colour as his skin and his eyes, the colour of mildew, of dust. And his clothes, too, all grey, dirty canvas sandals, flannel trousers, threadbare woollen cardigan, shrunk at the back, sagging into points in front. No shirt, his chest clothed with the same light grey hair as his ancient head.

There had been no letter from any Miss Maclean, no booking, she told him.

"Then I must use the telephone," he said, turning to shuffle off to his room. "Will you give me an outside line, please."

He would have liked to add, "And don't listen to my call," but he knew it would be useless to offend her and probably only spur her on to make the effort of arranging to eavesdrop. Better to say nothing. Her indolence and her newspaper might stop the impulse. Satisfying one's curiosity was worth just so much effort, no more.

His first call was to a shipping agency to discover when his niece was expected to arrive at Princeton. In four days' time, he was told. He had three days, then, to consider the whole situation. It should be enough. Except for the two telegrams.

He laid them side by side, near the telephone in his room. Both were signed George. Both announced imminent arrival, looking forward to seeing him. One from Venezuela, one from New York. Despatched that same morning. At approximately the same time. Intriguing, to say the least of it.

So intriguing that after a short interval Mr Wilberforce took up the telephone receiver again. Paula had taken him off the outside line. He asked to be put back, swearing mildly to himself. He ought to have called Gopal first. Now she would be sure to listen in. He had never before put in two calls one after the other. Never at Gardenia Lodge, that is to say.

To his relief a girl's voice answered, merely giving the

lawyer's office number. Mr Wilberforce said, "Wilberforce speaking. Put me straight through, please."

If it worked, Paula might be foxed. The girl answered, "Yes, sir. At once." It had worked.

"Henry," Mr Wilberforce said. "I've got to see you tomorrow afternoon. Can you manage it? I suppose around five."

"Are you sure you want to come down town, Ben?" the lawyer's voice answered. "Would it not be more convenient for me to call upon you?"

Henry Gopal, second generation immigrant San Fernandan from India, law graduate of Oxford, spoke with concern and affection. He had always been pro-British. His grandfather had held high office in the British Raj and been ruined by independence. His father had left India to serve in San Fernando, only to suffer a similar heartbreak. Young Henry, named after his father's closest Oxford friend, had studied law to achieve an independent career, only to find himself an object of suspicion and dislike, both with government and people, for his proved ability and too evident success.

"It would be no trouble at all," he urged.

"No, no," Mr Wilberforce insisted. His voice, raised to make himself heard in both his calls, was giving out. Soon, he knew, he would be speechless. "Five then, if you can manage it."

"A pleasure," Gopal assured him, hearing the tone weakening to a whisper. "I will be expecting you."

Mr Wilberforce hung up with a sigh. Nice chap, Henry, but not a patch on his father. That had been the one to take the plunge, get out before the worst of the troubles started, the grinding readjustment after the appalling blood bath. He'd been well out of it himself by then. Years out of it. In Venezuela, recommending San Fernando.

Venezuela. He glanced with renewed interest and some amusement at one of the two telegrams, still lying side by side at his elbow.

He swept them together, stuffed them into a trouser pocket

and locking his door behind him shuffled away to the lounge where the television flickered in the gloom, watched by two business men, the only other white residents, and Mrs Maria Mancini, wife of the hotel proprietor.

Mr Wilberforce bowed to her as he passed the sofa where she sat. She acknowledged his greeting but did not smile. She watched him move silently to his usual chair, watched him sink slowly into it and slowly put up his sandalled feet on another. She noted with her usual disgust that he wore no socks. He never wore socks. He was a dirty, broken-down, horrible old man. But he paid his bills so she could not persuade Luigi to send him away. She was half afraid of him, too. Not so much afraid as Paula and the other women. They thought he used spells to make them break things or fall over obstacles as they went about their work. They believed he had power to leave his body and return to it at will. He was their excuse, their bad luck excuse, all the time. It would not lift until he went away.

Maria Mancini would have used some means to compel him to go if she had known any. But she did not. Her family had shed those early superstitions, that tyrannical blight of the spirit, as they rose in the social scale. The wife of an hotel proprietor, even an hotel as reduced as the Gardenia Lodge now was, could not descend to potions, to leaf medicine, to symbols of destruction; to magic, in fact. So Mrs Mancini watched the television play, a very old American Western, with a politely calm expression of interest, while her feelings, boiling ceaselessly, viscously, with untiring malice, reduced Mr Wilberforce's image to a small lifeless core.

The old man was quite unaware of this. If he had known he would not have been much impressed. Many people had wished him ill in the course of his long life. Many had taken active steps to be rid of him, but without success. Where guns and knives had failed he did not much regard spells or other forms of magic. Poison he knew and respected. Especially in the countries of South America and the Caribbean, where plants grew in such terrifying abundance. Not in Princeton, however.

Not in the neglected garden of the Gardenia Lodge Hotel.

The two American business men rose at half-past seven, leaving the television story in the middle of its final sequence, the inevitable gun battle among the rocks. Mr Wilberforce stayed for the return to the town with the villain, dead, slung across the saddle of his led horse. Then the old man followed the others into the dining room.

Jim brought him the menu, delighted to find Mas'r Wilb was unusually hungry, prepared for a three course meal, with coffee to follow. At the end of it, clearing away the coffee cup he said, "You swim tonight, sah?"

"Later," Mr Wilberforce said. "When the moon is up."

"Him two day past the full," Jim protested. "That late, man. Very late, you know, sah."

"Do you mind?" the old man asked, with his rare smile.

"No. Not mind. For you, I thinking. Late and maybe cold."

"It's never cold, Jim. Warm as a bath—always."

It was a standard joke between them. Jim never minded the heat, though he did not expect to work in the middle hours of the day. Mr Wilberforce never minded the cold.

When the sky was dark blue and the moon at last showing above the mango tree beside the swimming pool, Mr Wilberforce, a thin ghostly figure in faded blue trunks, dressing gown and towel over his arm, walked slowly from his room, across the drive, across the deserted loggia to the swimming pool. The silence of midday was gone, replaced by the chirping, clicking, whining, whirring, hooting voices and noises of crickets, frogs, insects and other small creatures of the night.

Jim rose up to meet Mr Wilberforce as he reached the side of the pool. The waiter's dark body in dark red trunks was scarcely visible behind the blown-up rubber mattress he carried before him like a shield.

When the two met Jim moved to the deep end of the pool and, going down the steps until he was standing waist-high in the water, launched the rubber bed and held it close in to the side of the pool. The old man, going down the steps in his turn, dipped himself in the water, swam a few strokes out and back, then, wriggling himself on to the mattress, lay flat, looking up at the moon.

"O.K., Jim," he whispered.

With a strong push he was floated off into the middle of the pool. Jim climbed back up the steps, wrapped himself in his own towel and went away to one of the dressing rooms that stood along the edge of the water. This was where Mr Wilberforce had left his own gown and towel. Jim brought them out, sat down on his hunkers against the door of the dressing room and waited.

The old man lay still, watching the moon and the few light clouds that drifted slowly over it, from time to time splashing himself with water, occasionally paddling his floating bed with his hands. After about half an hour he raised both arms in the air. Jim, watching intently all the time, saw the signal at once and sprang up. He dived neatly off the side, reached the old man in a few strong strokes and without a word towed the mattress back to the steps.

Mr Wilberforce needed help to find his feet again, but Jim was practised and skilful. He came up behind the old man, the rubber bed supported on his back and held by one hand while with the other he held Mr Wilberforce's arm. At the top of the steps he dropped the mattress, took up the towel and wrapped it about the now shivering skeleton beside him.

"You not *cold*, Mas'r Wilb?" he asked, laughing hugely.

"Not a bit. Not cold. Tired, though."

Worried too, thought Jim. Those telegrams. And the letter. They shouldn't worry poor old Wilb, he thought, angry with the unknown inconsiderates. He put an arm over the thin shoulders, drawing the towel closer as he hung the dressing gown over it. A protecting gesture, a gesture of affection, of concern, that Mr Wilberforce found uncomfortably moving.

"Bed," he said, discovering more voice than usual. "I'm very much obliged to you, Jim. Don't deserve it."

He moved away from the protecting arm and without looking round or speaking again, went slowly to his room, unwinding from his wrist the key to it, which he wore day and night in that position, held in place by a broad band of elastic, like a bracelet with a charm attached.

Jim leaned the rubber bed against the door of the swimming pool cubicle, then followed. His black skin shone in the moonlight as he crossed the drive. The crickets chirped, the frogs whined. The night was busy, loud, alive, familiar. Mas'r Wilb had praised him. Jim was satisfied.

CHAPTER TWO

The first of Mr Wilberforce's visitors walked up the drive of the Gardenia Lodge Hotel just after nine the next morning. He was wearing a creased light grey suit of some cotton material, an open-necked shirt of a faded yellow colour and black and white crêpe-soled shoes. He was not tall but had broad shoulders and big hands and feet. He looked as if he had been meant to grow into a very big man but had been prevented in childhood from so doing. Which was precisely what had happened to him.

At the top of the drive he paused, looking first at the open door marked Office above the lintel and then at the shaded porch, where Mrs Mancini sat, fanning herself with a picture magazine. She returned his inquiring, hesitant look with a blank stare, so he walked over to the office door and peered into the gloom.

"Anyone about?" he demanded, in English, repeating the question almost at once in Spanish.

His voice was harsh, not loud, but carrying. Paula answered quietly in English, "Can I help you?"

She did not add, 'Sir' as she might have done a few years

back, before independence. If she knew the name, she used it, otherwise she left her remarks unaddressed.

"I've come to see Mr Wilberforce, who is staying here, I believe."

"Yes."

Paula still did not move. Mr Wilberforce had sent a message earlier that morning by Lizzie, who always took his morning coffee to his room. The message was to warn Paula of the arrival of a visitor early and perhaps another one later on. So this must be the early one. Just arrived from overseas, she decided. His crumpled suit smelled of oil and seaweed. To look so battered it must have been shut up in a drawer or in a suitcase too small for it. By its cut she guessed it was very old. The sort you noticed on television in old American films of the mid-fifties.

The visitor waited for some action that did not come, then said, with ill-concealed annoyance, "Well, if Mr Wilberforce is staying here, why don't you raise him on the blower and tell him I've arrived."

"What name, please?" Her calm, he saw, was indestructible. Her pale, smooth, sand-coloured skin was perfect, damn her.

"What name, please?" she repeated.

"Wilberforce. I told you."

"*Your* name, please?"

"Wilberforce, for God's sake!" Her momentary confusion, even alarm, was rewarding. "I'm Benedict Wilberforce's nephew, George Wilberforce," he said. He added, "He expects me," watching for some further emotional change to feed his revenge and his growing interest.

But Paula's face had resumed its usual blankness. However, she came forward, threw up the flap in the counter, passed through, said a few words over her shoulder and left the office. A shadow who had been sitting motionless behind a silent typewriter at the back of the office came forward at once to take her place.

The man who had announced himself as George Wilber-

force did not even glance at the substitute. He had waited until
Paula reached the drive, then followed swiftly, arriving just
behind her as she reached the old man's room. He had time to
notice, as he crossed the porch, that the staring woman had
disappeared.

Without turning, but showing she knew he was behind her
Paula said, "He gets up late. He may not be ready to receive
you."

She knocked at the door. They both listened. She knocked
again. This time a burst of cheerful laughter answered the
knock, but not from the room. It came from the corridor and
from the waiter, Jim, who walked towards them, his face still
open with mirth.

"Mas'r Wilb bin up an' dressed long time," he explained.
"Tell me he expect visitor. You visitor, sah?" he asked
politely, directing his gaze across Paula's shoulder.

"I have come to see my uncle," the stranger said, impatiently.
"If Mr Wilberforce has told you he expects me kindly take me
to him. At once."

Jim turned without a word and began to walk away along the
corridor. Paula, also silent, moved off in the opposite direction.
After a moment's hesitation the new arrival followed Jim.

Mr Wilberforce held out a hand in greeting but did not
leave his wicker armchair. He was in his usual place on the
flower-shaded verandah of the lounge.

"Well, George," he said, mildly, "it's been a long time. I
wouldn't have recognised you. Sit down. Coffee, or something
stronger?"

"Neither thank you, Uncle Ben. Too early for alcohol. I had
breakfast on board after we docked."

"You came by sea?"

"Freighter, yes. Worked my passage. Had to."

Jim was still hovering, waiting for orders. Mr Wilberforce
nodded to him to come closer.

"My usual coffee, Jim. Sure you won't have anything,
George? Something soft, perhaps? Long. Cold. I thought you

looked a bit tired—and dejected, perhaps, as you walked up the drive."

"You—*saw* me!"

George was confused; suddenly very angry. The decrepit object in the wicker armchair had taken him by surprise. Again. The long distant past surged up in his mind and heart, choking him.

"Why, yes," Uncle Ben said, with amusement. "Look behind you. Between the red bougainvillaea and the pink hibiscus. Where the grass ends, that's the drive. There! Where that car passed!"

"I see," George said, sulkily. "I had a devil of a time getting that girl in the office to bring me in."

"Bad luck," said Mr Wilberforce, blandly. "I sent Jim to find you when you didn't appear."

As if this brought his mind back to the waiter's continuing presence he said, looking at the apparently empty door of the lounge, "My coffee, Jim, and a planter's punch for Mr George."

The nephew threw up his hands, but yielded. There was something unexpected about Uncle Ben, something disturbing, to put it mildly. In the conversation he meant to have with him he would need all the nerve he could muster. A dose of rum might be very helpful.

If the punch helped at all it was in keeping the nephew's unwilling monologue flowing. Mr Wilberforce gave him no help. He listened politely, showing neither the resentment the other expected, nor the fear he relied upon.

When he had finished there was a long silence. Mr Wilberforce continued to sip his coffee at intervals. George, having finished the planter's punch, fiddled with the now bent straws in the glass, waiting.

At last, giving way to impatience, he barked in a loud, angry voice, "Well?"

"Well," said Mr Wilberforce, calmly. "I don't think *well* has any place in this. I think it is uniformly *ill*. I advise you to go away. To give up your silly plans. To go back to Venezuela and whoever induced you to try this stupid plot."

George was on his feet now, fumbling in his creased jacket pocket.

"Sit down!" said Uncle Ben, sharply. "You've had your turn, now it's mine."

The visitor subsided slowly.

"I wonder you had the nerve, apart from the folly, to come here like this," the old man continued. "Threatening me with the past. The very distant past. Do you really think the newspapers at home would take the slightest interest in hearing my brother George was a big-time crook and fraudulent embezzler. They got all the meat out of that subject more than twenty years ago."

"Possibly." The younger man turned an insolent face. "Out of him—my father—perhaps. Out of you, though? His trial and sentence broke you, didn't they? Even if they never brought a case against you as accessory."

"They couldn't. And I was not broken, you know. Did your father never tell you I was not broken, as you call it? Certainly I resigned my commission in the regular army, but I was still employed. Perhaps you were too young to be told this."

"I was not too young. Do you still say you have nothing to fear if I expose you? No interest to the Press at all? What about here, in independent San Fernando? What about Cuba?"

"You swine!" said Mr Wilberforce pleasantly. "So what do you propose?"

"You will assign to me, as from the end of this week, your coffee plantation here, the freehold of the land, the assets of the crop, the tourism at the hotel and so on. It will be a legal transaction. A contract. Drawn up properly by lawyers. After all, you are an old man, Uncle Ben. You can't have much longer to live. You don't look very well to me—"

He was going on in a desperate last attempt to break the other's resistance. But he was stopped by a simple question, twice repeated.

"A lawyer's agreement. Fair enough. What do you give me in return? I ask you. What do you give me in return?"

"Return for what?"

"For my property. A fair price. How much?"

"I've told you. My silence."

"I don't give a damn for your silence. What proof have you got? If anyone cared, which I say again I very much doubt. Don't you think any respectable, reputable lawyer, such as the one I use here, will want to be very sure what he's handling before drawing up a simple deed of gift. What's to prevent me going with the whole story to the police? Blackmail has a very strong, distinguishable smell, you know."

That stung. Once more George got to his feet, this time to turn away, making for the edge of the verandah, the lawn and the drive beyond.

"I'm sorry to disappoint you—Manfred," called Mr Wilberforce.

The retreating back stiffened as if a bullet had struck it. But the face that looked round at the old man was puzzled, even shocked.

"*What* did you call me?" the man said.

"You heard. Come back here."

Uncle Ben took some currency notes from his pocket.

"My turn again," he said. "You will go back to your ship tonight and to Venezuela when she sails tomorrow. Yes, I know she will sail tomorrow. D'you think I haven't known all these years where you were, the pair of you? Who tipped you off to find me here?"

There was no answer. Nor did the stranger come nearer to take the notes, so Mr Wilberforce returned them to his pocket.

"Very well," he said. "Go your own way, but don't try any more silly ploys. You can't bounce me, you know."

"You recognised—?" The voice had grown deeper with a guttural note carelessly uttered.

"Not really. You were only nine, I think. No, your bad luck. I had another telegram yesterday, also signed George. From the States. More likely, really, don't you think? Brother George went there when they let him out. Joined his wife and the boy, after he'd picked up the saltings on the continent. You still don't care to—?" He held out the notes again.

"Damn you to hell!" said the other in a low growl and went away, walking uncertainly over the rough grass of the lawn and down the bank to the drive. His head appeared again, moving towards the road, then he was gone.

At once Jim appeared with a tray to clear away the cup and the glass.

"You saw that man?" whispered Mr Wilberforce, whose voice was now collapsing to its usual level. "Not my nephew George Wilberforce. Name is Manfred Stein. Remember that, Jim. Manfred Stein."

Jim nodded solemnly and went away, practising the name. Manfrey Stine. Manfry Shine. Manfy Zine.

The two American business men were surprised to find Mr Wilberforce at lunch that day in the dining room of the hotel. They remarked upon it afterwards.

"The guy was really eating for once," the younger one said, as he climbed behind the wheel of their car in the drive.

"He had a visitor this morning, Jim told me," answered the other. "Seems like he was stimulated, somehow. Relative, Jim said."

The other grinned and nodded.

"Maybe so. Shook me seeing the old boy get outside all those calories. Like meeting a ghost chewing a T-bone steak."

"You keep your eye on the highway, boy, or we'll make town as ghosts ourselves. Ain't no traffic rules apply in this island."

Mr Wilberforce, unaware of the interest he had aroused, lay on his bed after lunch. But he did not sleep. He was waiting for the second George Wilberforce to make his appearance.

This happened at three o'clock, when a well-polished American car of some eight years' vintage drove into the hotel. Before the driver had time to get out of it Mr Wilberforce left his room and moved on to the porch leading from the corridor.

He was able to get a clear view of the stranger before the latter saw him. So, also, was Mrs Mancini, peeping round the curtain of her own front door that opened off the porch on the side nearest the kitchens.

"Your own car, George?" Mr Wilberforce asked, pleasantly, from the shadow of the porch.

The man wheeled round. He had noticed the office opposite as he came to the sweep of the drive. He had continued to look at it as he switched off his engine and eased himself backwards from the driving seat. He had not expected to meet his uncle without being announced. He was considerably disconcerted.

"Your own car, George?" Mr Wilberforce repeated, smiling now, enjoying the situation.

"Hired," answered the newcomer sulkily. "Just flew into Montserrat Bay airfield. Arranged the hire last week."

"I got your wire only yesterday."

"I sent it yesterday."

They looked at each other, careful, assessing, controlled.

"Well, if the car's only hired, perhaps you'd like to pull back into the shade under the swimming pool wall over there. Better for it in this heat, don't you think? And lock it up, won't you? I'll wait here."

With no alternative, the newcomer took these suggestions. He told himself for the hundredth time that day that he must play it cool. On no account annoy the old boy. Mustn't show him he had the whip hand. Not to begin with, anyhow.

"He thought he had the whip hand of me," Mr Wilberforce explained to Henry Gopal that evening. "The second George, I mean."

"You really think he is your brother's son?" the Indian asked, with a puzzled frown. "It is a most strange coincidence. After all these years—on the same day."

"Don't say it," Mr Wilberforce begged him. "Nothing is stranger than reality. Don't forget Lucy's letter. He must have known she'd warn me he was coming. Or might come. He was not surprised when I told him so."

"You really have identified him, then?" the lawyer insisted. "You are sure this American-speaking stranger is George Wilberforce's son?"

"Unless he found a double in the States. In which case he'd be dead. This isn't a proposition to share with a partner. Not the way he proposed to work it."

"Tell me."

"He declared quite positively that his father, my brother the crook, had shared the proceeds of his last haul, the last English one, that is, when he got twelve years, with me and that I have the loot, my half share, cached away on my coffee plantation here. He seems to be quite convinced of it. Says his father told him on oath it was true just before he died."

Mr Gopal stared at his desk, digging into small holes in it with the ball point pen he held.

"He must be a stupid as well as a greedy man," he said. "Unlike his father, who was never stupid."

"But always greedy, you mean?" said Mr Wilberforce. "No, George was stupid, too. Working on the scale he did he ought to have known he'd not get away with it more than twice at most. Stupid, cunning, courageous, self-confident, totally self-regarding. He ought to have broken his neck on the first job he did. Better for him and all the rest of us if he had."

"That was when he climbed a half-demolished house to get into the empty one next door and from its cellar into the bank on the corner?"

"Yes."

Mr Wilberforce resented the half admiring note in the Indian's voice.

"You don't agree with me?"

Mr Gopal spread out his hands.

"Of course I agree. It's just that a rebel, all rebels, particularly very daring young men, have a certain appeal—"

"Not to their unfortunate relations," Mr Wilberforce reminded him. "George ruined my army career. Damned nearly ruined my subsequent one. And now this young lout comes along, threatening me with exposure."

"Like the other one."

"More or less. But American George is prepared to wait. What he demands is that I make a new will leaving the estate to him, together with precise instructions, deposited, sealed, at my bank, giving him the exact location of the loot."

Mr Gopal's large dark eyes blazed with excitement, mixed with incredulity.

"But—but my dear Benedict, this is incredible! I did not imagine you were speaking of anything but investments. This man thinks you have *treasure—buried treasure*—what, for instance?"

"I haven't the faintest idea."

"You—you didn't *ask* him what he thought your brother had given you, how, where, when—"

"I did not. I simply said he had no claim on my estate. He might be George's heir, but he is not my next of kin, as my sister Lucy is alive and well, in England. Not to mention her daughter, my niece. But I didn't tell him Alison was coming here. I rather wish she wasn't. But I can't prevent it, as she's on the way. I hope he'll have gone before she arrives."

There was not much time, he remembered, frowning. Perhaps Henry—But the lawyer was still unsatisfied.

"Did you not want to know what he meant by this—loot? This supposed treasure?"

"No. Since it does not exist as far as I am concerned."

"There must be some reason for this man's belief, must there not? Something his father told him, or believed. Not what he says. Something he has twisted into this fantasy of buried treasure."

Mr Wilberforce looked away into the distance, his face quite without expression. It was a look the solicitor was accustomed to in this country of mixed races, a look based on caution, or fear, or withdrawal; of accepted non-understanding of alien thought, alien culture—often of plain dislike—but above all of the refusal, the total avoidance of conflict, unless provoked beyond endurance.

Mr Gopal said, gently, "You must forgive my curiosity, Ben. Is there anything you wish me to do for you? Beyond taking down a note of this story of a threat?"

Mr Wilberforce turned back to his friend with a laugh of genuine pleasure.

"Of course. My sister has a will, or rather a copy of a will I made the last time I was in England, years ago. She may have lost it, or thrown it away. She can't think I have anything to leave her. It was in her favour though, in trust for her daughter. I want you now to get out a new one, in those same terms, but with one small legacy added. To be paid in cash. To Jim Hulbert. He's the sole remaining waiter at the Gardenia Lodge. A very good waiter. Much more than a waiter to me. A friend."

He paused, watching Gopal write down these instructions.

"Can you get this ready for me to sign quite soon? Say, tomorrow at this time?"

Mr Gopal looked disturbed.

"Is it so urgent? Is there danger? From one of these two men? From both? The police—"

"No," said Mr Wilberforce, "definitely not the police. Do your best, Henry. I'll come in again this time tomorrow unless you phone to say you're not ready."

They shook hands, as they always did, warmly, but with a certain formality. Mr Gopal went to the street door with his friend and client, saw him hail a taxi, watched him drive away. He went back to his office in a thoughtful mood. Benedict had had a strange story to tell and had left out most of it, he decided. But he had his instructions. He would be ready with the will to sign and the proper witnesses by the next day in the afternoon.

Mr Wilberforce appeared at dinner at the hotel that evening. He took some soup, but refused the next two courses. He left the table after drinking a small cup of coffee. The Americans were disappointed to note the old man's relapse. Starving himself again.

When Jim went to Mr Wilberforce's room later that evening, to carry the rubber mattress to the swimming pool, he found him still dressed, sitting at his table, writing.

"No bathe tonight, Jim," he said, without turning his head. "Thank you for calling. Goodnight."

CHAPTER THREE

Mr Wilberforce took coffee and toast in his room the next morning at eight and at nine called for a taxi to drive him to the University Hospital.

This was his usual Tuesday routine; he had postponed it one day on account of the two callers, but this caused no stir of any kind at Gardenia Lodge. Mr Wilberforce kept the taxi waiting for five minutes, then emerged in a very old-fashioned yellowed version of tropical uniform for officers of the British Army. It was considerably too large for him in his present emaciated state, but it was an improvement on his usual grey outfit. Besides, the hospital records had him described as Colonel Wilberforce; the staff there addressed him by that title.

He was not kept waiting. In Out-patients the Sister, wide, motherly, very black, very competent, took him off to a dressing room as soon as he appeared in her department. When he came out, looking thinner and greyer than ever in a long hospital dressing gown, she led him past several rows of waiting patients to a door marked Staff and throwing it open made way for him to pass her, then followed him in.

"The Colonel, sir," she said and retreated.

The room, a small annex of the consulting room, with wash-basins, sterilisers, examination apparatus of various kinds, had in addition been furnished this morning with a small table and two chairs. The man seated in one of these rose as Mr Wilberforce entered.

"Good morning, Colonel," he said, cheerfully. "I was expecting you yesterday, but this is quite O.K. Everything all right?"

"Of course not," answered the old man, with a certain contempt for the other's manner. "I should have thought you'd know by this time I've one foot in the grave and the other itching to join it."

Not at all disconcerted Dr Grigg said, "We don't expect outpatients to have such a clear picture of their condition."

He laughed, to imply that his joke was as good as the other's but cut it off when he saw a slight flush of anger stain the wrinkled face before him.

"Something's happened," he said, altogether serious now. "What is it?"

Mr Wilberforce did not answer, but merely turned his head a little to say, "Thank you, Sister," in a dismissing tone of voice.

She smiled, knowing the colonel's ways, she thought. Dr Grigg repeated, "Thank you, Sister," reinforcing the colonel. She left the room at once.

"Now go ahead," said Dr Grigg.

When he had heard the news, bothering for the old boy, of course, but hardly his own business to interfere in, he made as careful an examination of his patient's heart and lungs as was possible in the sitting position. He was not satisfied.

"I'll have to have you on the couch this week," he said, briskly. "Stay where you are while I clear the next room. She ought to be dressed by now."

Having disposed of this problem Dr Grigg called the nurse in the consulting room, despatched her to fetch in Colonel Wilberforce and set about preparing to take electrocardiograph readings, besides looking up the results of former tests and X-rays. When his full examination had been completed he stood, quite silent, looking down at his patient.

"Well?" said Mr Wilberforce. "Worse, isn't it?"

"I'm afraid so."

"I'm not. Afraid, I mean. Expected it. Heart or arteries?"

Dr Grigg lifted his shoulders slowly and dropped them with a jerk.

"The lot," he said. "Wear and tear, as I've told you before. After all you've told me about your life it's not surprising, even if only fifty per cent of your stories are true."

"Seventy-five," said Mr Wilberforce, with the suggestion of a grin. "Anything to be done about it? I mean, I don't really mind when I hand in my chips. But with Alison coming here—And those two still about—Perhaps more, trailing *them*—"

His voice faded into silence. But he roused himself to ask, "What can I do to keep going a bit longer?"

"How much longer? Years, I should say, are out. Months—Depends how you look after yourself. Avoid physical effort. Avoid emotional scenes. Don't lose your temper. Remember John Hunter. 'My life is at the mercy of any wretch who angers me.' His aneurysm burst and killed him in the end, precisely because he lost his temper."

"Aneurysm, is it? I see. Rest and tranquillity. I'll do what I can. But it won't be easy, you know."

"I don't suppose it will—for a man like you. It's the best I can offer."

"I appreciate that."

Dr Grigg pulled a prescription pad nearer. He wrote quickly, tore off the page, handed it to Mr Wilberforce.

"It might help to take these, Colonel," he said. "One every morning instead of the ones you've been on all this year so far."

"Thank you. I can get them here at the dispensary?"

"Certainly."

The consultation was at an end. The nurse opened the door for him, his successor was beckoned in. Sister forestalled the newcomer to tell Dr Grigg she had put another special case in the little room. The doctor hurried away to attend to it.

When he was dressed again Mr Wilberforce found his own way to the dispensary. The pharmacist, an old acquaintance, was multiracial in appearance; something in his high cheek-bones and copper-coloured skin suggested the Amerindian, though his mouth and nose were European. He nodded gravely when he saw the fresh prescription.

"Dr Grigg is not so pleased with you."

"So it seems."

"I am very sorry, Colonel. So you will not see Dr Grigg again."

Mr Wilberforce looked genuinely startled.

"Heh! Does that mean he expects me to kick the bucket in under a *week*?"

The dispenser laughed heartily.

"No, no! Oh, dear me, no! Dr Grigg is going back to England. His year is up. Didn't he tell you so?"

"No. He didn't tell me."

Mr Wilberforce was frowning. Why had Grigg not mentioned his going? Afraid of upsetting him? Wasn't it more upsetting to be startled by the news—as now? He controlled his sudden anger, feeling his heart begin to pound uncomfortably. He said, careful to speak slowly, "Will there be a replacement from England? Otherwise, who will take over my case?"

"Another Britisher, yes, Colonel. Again, for a year. We have these young men in all departments, you know. Very valuable experience—for them as for us."

"I don't doubt it," Mr Wilberforce said. "Do you know his name? He is here now, I suppose, if he is to take over next week."

"Oh yes, Colonel. Dr Faulkner. From London University and St Edmund's Hospital in London. He has been here six months now. Both he and Dr Stone, who comes from the States."

"Dr Stone?" asked Mr Wilberforce, slowly.

"The radiologist. Yes. I think you saw him when Dr Grigg sent you for a fresh X-ray about three weeks ago."

"Yes," Mr Wilberforce answered, nodding gravely. "Yes. It must have been Dr Stone."

He drove back to the hotel in a very thoughtful frame of mind. Agitated too, but he tried to argue himself out of that.

To begin with, the pharmacist's wide knowledge of hospital doings, changes of staff, treatment of patients. Of course the man had to check the patients' notes to sign the register for drugs. But why concern himself with X-ray tests? Did his curiosity extend to all patients? Or was it reserved for a few, even for himself, alone? Why? And for what ultimate purpose? Reward? Again why, and from whom?

Mr Wilberforce grew calmer. The position was perfectly clear. He wanted to see Alison. She was due to arrive on the next day or the one after. But the two Georges, one of them being not George, but Manfred, would be coming again to see him before she arrived, to pester him. He could not afford to be pestered, annoyed, perhaps threatened, this time more openly, more urgently, more dangerously. There was only one thing to do, he decided, sighing.

It was lunch time when the taxi arrived back at the Gardenia Lodge. Mr Wilberforce passed through the empty dining room to the verandah outside the lounge. On the way he whispered to Jim to bring him a pot of tea and a sandwich outside.

"Cooler here with conditioning on, sah," Jim told him. "Very good lunch. Paw-paw. You'se like paw-paw, Mas'r Wilb."

"Add some to the sandwich," Mr Wilberforce said, continuing on his way.

Mrs Mancini, who found the deserted dining room very depressing, spoke about it to her husband when he joined her there.

"Why don't we leave?" she said. "A year ago, nine months ago, you said you'd had enough. God knows I have. What's keeping you?"

"Him," Mancini answered, with a sideways nod towards the lounge and the verandah.

"Old Wil—"

"Sh—" Mancini silenced her with a fierce gesture. Leaning forward over the table he began speaking in the language they used together, when they did not want to be understood by others; a language made up of his faulty Italian, her hybrid Spanish and an assortment of words from the local English patois.

"It is important for me to keep him here until—until—"

"For the rest of his life, you mean?"

"Just that. We know he is ill, that he has a heart disease. He has told Jim he will not live for ever. His way of saying he does not expect to live much longer."

"That is your interpretation. If his life is to be so short what is the point of our waiting for him to die? The money for his room will not be a fortune for just a few weeks."

"The money from the insurance will be. A very nice little fortune."

Mrs Mancini was startled.

"Insurance? What insurance? You have never told me of any insurance!"

"I do not tell you all my business, Maria. There are things beyond—"

"Beyond my understanding! You need not repeat that old lie! I have enough understanding to know that insurance companies do not insure lives that are old and diseased like his."

"This one did."

"Then it must be a crook firm. No real firm with real money would do it. Or you have lied on the form. You have put him down as healthy, when the death certificate will say heart disease."

"Not if he dies of an accident," said Mancini carefully. "I have made the insurance for accident only."

Mrs Mancini was horrified. She threw up her hands, knocking them against the table so that the crockery rattled and Jim appeared at the door of the lounge, a look of grave concern on his face.

"Finish your lunch, Maria," said Mancini in English. "Jim wants to clear the table."

As the pair moved out of the dining room into the lounge they met Mr Wilberforce coming slowly towards them from the verandah. He bowed politely to Mrs Mancini, waiting for her to pass into the corridor in front of him. He followed directly after her, causing Mancini himself to bring up the rear. Also he walked slowly, allowing the hotel owner's wife to move out of sight before he reached the door of his room. There he paused, looked round and said, "Can I have a word with you, Mancini? In here, if you like. Or in the office. On business."

In the office there would be Paula, Mancini thought. She knew English well, British English, whereas he always found Mr Wilberforce's speech particularly difficult. But Paula was inquisitive; also the office was very near the loggia where there were still a few remaining guests of a Fernandan lunch party, chattering and laughing loudly.

So he walked into Mr Wilberforce's room where he had not been for several months and took the chair the old man offered him.

Mr Wilberforce, still standing, said in his husky voice, "I may be leaving here very soon, Mr Mancini. I may not be able to give you proper notice, but—"

"You have to give me one month!" Mancini burst out, before the other had time to stop him.

The old man sighed. He had known his landlord would be tiresome. He saw that he would not only be tiresome, but an obstinate bore as well. However.

"We are on weekly terms," he said. "Fixed last year by my—agent here when he arranged to take a room for me. I would like to pay my bill for the four, or is it five, weeks owing. And I will add another week's money on deposit. Then if I want to leave at short notice my account outstanding will be negligible and easy to tot up? Am I right?"

Mancini considered this far from right. A comparatively small, but fixed source of income was threatened by an old man's whim. An old sick man. Mancini had long ago made plans for Mr Wilberforce's expected collapse. He knew exactly how to get in touch with a reliable doctor. Reliable from his own point of view, that is. One who would see that the old man did not suffer, who had already agreed to the modest ten per cent rake-off Mancini offered. Similarly with a nurse. The form of the collapse? Time and the occasion would dictate that, so long as it could be pronounced an accident. Not a gross accident. Just something that a young strong man would recover from, but an old frail one would not.

These plans and the insurance contingent on them, so carefully, so laboriously thought out, might now be torn to bits by a whim, an old man's whim.

"It is not that I am unhappy here or at all uncomfortable," said Mr Wilberforce, who had watched with amusement the expressions of surprise, dismay, frustrated greed and anger pass over the olive lined face of his landlord. "You must not think I am at all dissatisfied. It is just that I wish to be— prepared."

Mancini remembered the taxi of that morning.

"The hospital! Your doctor there has frightened you? He has disclosed something? Warned of something?"

"You could say that—in a way," Mr Wilberforce agreed.

Mancini felt relief. His guest's mysterious illness, of which he never spoke at all intelligibly, must be reaching a crisis. Very well. It was a situation he could handle.

"I understand, Colonel Wilberforce," he said, using the title the man had given when he first came to Gardenia Lodge, but which no one there had ever used since. "I will go across to the office and bring back your account immediately. To your room. Please to have your rest now."

Mr Wilberforce thanked him, watched him go and locked his door behind him. He had meant what he said about Gardenia Lodge. A comfortable room, if shabby; excellent food; welcome solitude. He lay down on his bed, wondering when the two Georges would appear again and which would come first.

It was the bogus nephew, as he had really expected all along. The other, who might very well really be George's son, was prepared to wait. Following in George's footsteps. Vague threats, uncomfortable suspense, unreasoning fear. Mr Wilberforce chuckled quietly to himself. This time there could be no fear. Henry Gopal would see to that—and other matters. Mr Wilberforce turned on his side and slept.

He was woken by Jim, who came knocking at the door. He brought an importantly large envelope from Mancini and announced that: "Mas'r George Wilb, him you say is Man—Man—Stee—"

"Manfred Stein," Mr Wilberforce corrected, "pronounced Stine," he added, gently. "Yes. I expected him. You've put him on the verandah?"

"Yes, sah. I bring tea?"

"In ten minutes, yes please, Jim."

When the waiter had gone Mr Wilberforce opened the envelope. His bill, up to date, was set out on a Gardenia Lodge hotel account form dating from the time of some previous owner called Lionel Thompson. Probably Mancini had never bothered to get his own name on the bill heads. Possibly Thompson had left too hurriedly in the end, leaving stocks of printed stationery. And this had been used up far too slowly, so that, even now, there was plenty left.

Mr Wilberforce glanced rapidly at the bill, then wrote out a cheque for the full amount, put both cheque and account back in the envelope, fastened it and, letting himself out of his room very quietly, took it over to the office, where he handed it to Paula.

He then walked up the path under the bougainvillaeas to

the verandah where he expected to find his guest. There was no one there.

But as he went in, walking through to the lounge, he met Jim, who at once explained.

"He say he not stay. Then he went over to swim pool. Said he wait there till you come."

"I see," said Mr Wilberforce, calmly. "I'd better go after him."

He walked away across the lawn, across the drive, through the now empty loggia, shaded by its mango trees, to the sun-drenched swimming pool beyond. George, whom he thought of as Manfred, was there, sitting on the pale blue tiles that surrounded the pool, with his back against a changing cubicle.

"I'm sorry to keep you waiting," Mr Wilberforce said, politely. "But after all, I have nothing to say to you. I refused to give you money before, except perhaps for your expenses in coming to see me, and I still refuse. You can spread any slander or libel about me that occurs to you. I shan't care. So go now. There is no point in arguing. I shan't change my mind."

"I'll go when I choose."

The man had lost his earlier placatory, faintly cringing air. His face now wore a truculent expression.

"I'll go when I choose," he repeated, "after you've given me what I asked you for."

"Not a penny," Mr Wilberforce said, firmly. "Not even for expenses, now. Nothing."

He stood for a few seconds looking down at the man, dirty, ill-clothed, who lolled against the closed door of the changing cubicle. Then he turned and shuffled slowly back to his room, meeting Jim at the entrance to the corridor.

"Tea for one in my room, Jim," he said. "I shall not see that visitor if he comes again."

"You send him away?" Jim asked, grinning delightedly.

"He is his own master," answered the old man, quietly.

Late that evening the usual procession moved from the

hotel room towards the swimming pool, Mr Wilberforce, in his dressing gown this time, carrying his towel, Jim behind, wearing swimming trunks only, with the inflated rubber mattress in his arms.

Mr Wilberforce, as usual, went to the changing cubicle to put down his towel and take off his dressing gown. But this time he came out again, still wearing the gown.

"Jim," he said, hurriedly, in a voice raised above his usual whisper, "I have forgotten something very important. No, nothing you can *fetch*. Something you must *take*. A letter. It should have gone this afternoon."

He had taken the rubber mattress from the astonished waiter's arms and put it down on the tiles beside the pool. He had taken Jim by the arm and was leading him back to the hotel, walking fast and talking as they went.

"A short note, but it must be delivered tonight. At once. You will take it for me? Of course you will. I'll write it now. You have only to ring the bell and give the envelope to Mr Gopal, who will answer the door himself, I expect."

Jim, thoroughly confused by all this, watched and waited with no very clear idea of what exactly he was to do. Even when he had the letter in its envelope, directed, addressed, thrust into his hand, with a final brief order to get on a shirt and trousers and hurry, he stood, turning the message over and over and repeating, "How you swim, Mas'r Wilb? How you get in the water? How you get out?"

"Oh, never mind that, Jim." The old man was exasperated. "I'll manage. I'll tie the mattress to the steps with a length of string. Then I can pull myself back when I want to get out. Quite simple. Now get a move on, my dear chap. Hurry!"

Jim had never been called a dear chap before, but he was a simple, straightforward person, so he rightly took it as a mark of affection, not as an insult, and did as he was told.

He had no difficulty in finding Mr Gopal's house. The door was opened by a brown-faced boy, who promised to take the note straight to his master.

"There will be an answer?" he asked, in his clipped, precise English.

"Mas'r Wilb no say 'bout any answer," Jim said, looking at the boy's thin, clever face with disfavour. The door was shut again immediately.

On his way back to Gardenia Lodge Jim considered these strange happenings. Mas'r Wilb had gone out again after tea. Where to? He had thought it was to see Mr Gopal. But that could not be if he now sent him a letter. It was very confusing.

Meeting a friend in the road as he was returning Jim was persuaded to join this man for a drink. Others came, more drinks circulated. Jim did not get back to the hotel for three hours from the time he had left.

It was now past midnight. The late moon, very thin, very low now in the sky, gave a pallid light over the swimming pool when Jim walked up there to bring in the used rubber mattress. He expected to find it on the side of the pool, or even still tied to the steps. It was not in either place. Peering over the water, Jim could not see it anywhere.

He stared and stared. He walked round the edge of the large rectangle, still staring at the water. He looked into the changing cubicle. Mr Wilberforce's towel and dressing gown were there on the bench. The towel was dry.

With a sickening fear in his heart Jim tore off his clothes and dived into the water. He swam up and down several times, finding nothing. He was looking for the mattress, a large enough object to come across, he thought, if you were near enough and at the right level. But he found nothing and swam back towards the steps. Too much drink, he was thinking now. He hadn't really seen that dry towel, that old dressing gown. Mas'r Wilb had carried the mattress back himself. Why hadn't he looked for it first at the hotel? Mas'r Wilb had been asleep these several hours.

He found himself looking into the face of Mr Wilberforce, there beside him in the water. Asleep all right, eyes closed in the old, grey, wrinkled face, the water washing gently over it and across the thin closed lips. Asleep now for eternity.

In sudden terror Jim drew in a breath half water, choked, lashed out with his arms, felt the body below the face, floundered past it to the steps, almost incapable of swimming and collapsed at the top of them, weak, breathless, shaking, but safe.

He had drowned Mas'r Wilb. If indeed he was dead. Yes, of course he was dead. The body had been cold. And stiff. Drowned. He had drowned because he, Jim, had not hurried back from his mission, but had gone drinking with friends. Drowned him because he had not insisted upon looking after Mas'r Wilb instead of obeying his crazy whim, instead of persuading him to give up his bathe for that once. He remembered the old man had not bathed the night before.

So now, what to do? Rouse Mr Mancini, who was a devil when he was disturbed? Rouse the other servants? They would be crazy with fear. So would his wife, Therese. Paula did not live at Gardenia Lodge. No one would touch the body. The spell that had taken Mas'r Wilb off his mattress and taken the mattress right away would still be powerful in the body. He had nearly drowned, himself. He remembered the sudden effort, the dreadful pull of the water, of the drowned body really, as he had struggled to the steps, his fearful weakness as he dragged himself out to safety.

So Jim did nothing at all that night. He took up his clothes and went to his room. Therese was asleep, snoring gently. He rubbed himself dry, slipped into bed beside her and lay staring into the darkness, while silent tears of remorse and grief ran from his eyes and nose into the fold of sheet he held against his quivering mouth.

CHAPTER FOUR

The body was discovered by the old gardener, who had been sent up to the swimming pool to skim fallen leaves off the water. Leaves and insects fell into the pool daily. Once a week the gardener passed a wide shrimping net across as much of it as he could reach from the side. Once a fortnight the water was emptied away, the rest of the rubbish cleared out and fresh water run in.

The gardener was as horrified as Jim had been by the sight, floating in the water, of a grey face that he recognised. But he was less fearful than the waiter. He ran back to the hotel bawling for Mancini and told his tale with difficulty, being out of breath as well as agitated. Mancini, however, gathered the gist of it and immediately telephoned for the police. He then called for Jim.

The waiter, who had only just got out of bed, came running as soon as he had struggled into the legs of his pyjamas.

"Did Mr Wilberforce bathe last night?" Mancini asked sternly.

"He did so, man," Jim answered, steadily. He had decided upon his story after a night of anguish and found no difficulty now in telling it. "He go to bathe and then he change his mind."

"So he didn't bathe? What you saying? He bathe or he not bathe?"

"I tell you," Jim said patiently. "He had letter to write and send. I took it because he could not wait for post, he say."

"Did he bathe or did he not bathe?"

"Mas'r Wilb say he go back to bathe. He would tie his rubber float to the steps and not need any help."

"You took the letter. Into the town, was it?"

"Yes, Mas'r Mancini."

The latter wanted to know where his servant had gone with a message so urgent it had to be delivered by hand. Late at night. But he controlled his curiosity.

"You did not go to the pool when you came back?"

"No, sah." Jim spoke calmly, without undue emphasis.

"Did you go to his room to tell him you had finished your errand?"

"No, sah. Mas'r Wilb trusted me."

In spite of his preparation Jim's eyes filled with tears at this thought.

Mrs Mancini appeared on the small verandah. She was wearing a frilled pink nylon housecoat. Her black hair hung in an untidy mass about her cream-skinned face and neck.

"All this *talk*!" she cried. "Lucky we have no guests now. Six in the morning. Are you crazy?"

Mancini wheeled round to face her.

"No guests? What you mean?"

"Those Americans checked out an hour ago. You sleep so sound you hear nothing. I heard. I say goodbye. They take their car. They pay their check."

Mancini was furious.

"They tell me nothing."

"They tell Paula last night. The check was pushed under their door this morning, they say."

"Paula did that?"

"How do I know? Paula not here yet."

Mancini put both hands to his head. Maria was impossible. He faced ruin.

He remembered the body in the pool. Mr Wilberforce, the gardener said. If so—an accident—his spirits leaped up at once.

"Go Jim," he ordered. "See if we have here a mistake. See if Mr Wilberforce is in his room."

Quaking with sudden terror, but not daring to show it, Jim went into the dark corridor and knocked at the old man's door.

No answer. He knocked again, more loudly, at the same time turning the handle and pushing.

To his intense surprise the door opened. He nearly fell into the room. The curtains were closed, the air conditioning was off, the bed was empty, still made up, but showing a dent on the pillow and coverlet where Mr Wilberforce had lain, fully dressed, taking his wakeful siesta.

Jim, who had gone only one step into the room, retreated backwards, feeling for the door handle behind him. He missed it, but found the key fitted in the hole on the inside. Leaving the door open he ran out again to his master.

Mancini, pleased with this confirmation of an accident, visited the room in his turn. He decided that he had better not touch anything. The police would be here soon, they might look for fingerprints. He went outside again, leaving the key on the inside of the door.

It was not long before a black car rolled up the drive. Three figures, smartly dressed in black with red sashes and red bands on their uniform caps sat for a few seconds without moving, a police inspector on the back seat, a constable driving and another sitting beside him. Mancini went forward as the inspector left the car.

"You made this report?" asked the inspector, briskly. "A man drowned in your swimming pool. I don't see an ambulance."

Mancini explained the situation as fully as he knew it, pushing forward the gardener, who was most unwilling to describe once again his unsettling experience.

"So you have no idea when this happened?" the inspector asked Mancini.

"No, man. No, Mr—"

"Vincent. Chief-Inspector Vincent."

"No, Mr Vincent. But, as I explained—"

"Show me this pool," the inspector demanded, looking round the multiracial group before him. He was a full-blooded negro himself and proud of it. He had joined the force early, had been praised and rewarded before independence, which, very secretly, he regretted. Politics had crept in everywhere since the old days. It was inevitable in a growing State, but he foresaw no further promotion for himself as things were now.

The group moved away to the pool, the police keeping the unwilling Mr Mancini close to them, all the hotel servants, collected now and assembled in the drive, shivering with fear and excitement, some paces behind. All that is to say except Paula, who, recently arrived, calm-faced as usual, said she would stay in the office to take phone calls.

The procession reached the pool. The dead man's face, lying just below the surface, not far from the shady side, was partly covered now by a big leaf from one of the surrounding trees. His body, submerged, was a vague shadow in the unclear depths of the water. Inspector Vincent turned to the gardener.

"We must get him out. You have a pole?"

The old man shook his head, but turned away and stooped to a long slender stick with a large net, spread on twigs like a shrimping net, fastened to it.

"You move him to steps, sah?" he suggested, offering this implement.

The inspector passed it to the constable, who had gone with him to the pool, leaving the driver in the car. "Get him to the end of the pool," the inspector went on and moved away before his subordinate could protest. Looking back over his shoulder, he added, "If you can't manage it you'll have to go in after him." Then beckoning to Jim he said, "You used to help him when he bathed, I believe. Show me where he left his things."

Jim was only too pleased to turn away from the water. He opened the door of the end cubicle. Inside, Mr Wilberforce's towel and dressing gown lay where they always had, neatly folded and placed on the single plank bench. The inspector picked them up, shook out the towel, unfolded the dressing gown and holding it by the collar felt in the pockets. There was a handkerchief in one, nothing in the other.

"The key of his room was in his door, man," he reminded Inspector Vincent. "Inside of door. Door unlocked, you know, Mas'r Wilb never left door unlocked. Always carried key on his arm, tied on."

He indicated a place just above his own wrist on the left side.

"Are you sure of that?"

"Out or in he lock his door," Jim answered, earnestly. "Man, I never knew that door open 'cept Mas'r Wilb he coming out or going in."

The constable came hurrying to the cubicle.

"Getting him out now, sir," he said, breathless with importance. "Bad sight, sir. Women upset."

"Take these," the inspector said, handing him the dressing gown and towel. "You," he added to Jim, "go to his room and bring out the sheets off his bed. We don't want the public coming in off the road. Hurry!"

Jim ran away back to the hotel, still keeping his face away from the pool and the still form he knew was lying on the edge now, near the steps. He brushed past his wife Therese, the three room maids, Paula's assistant in the office, all of whom were now moaning on a high-pitched note, swaying to and fro in the first onset of hysteria.

"Send your staff away," Inspector Vincent said, walking back to Mancini's side. The little hotel proprietor's face had taken on a more greenish tinge than usual. He was staring at the corpse, now decently covered, except for the face, by the spread towel and dressing gown.

"This is the Mr Wilberforce who was staying here," he asked, "You recognise him?"

Mr Mancini nodded miserably. The accident. The longed for, planned for, accident. Had it happened too soon? Would the insurance company have suspicions? This was all too ironical. He never meant it to be now, nor in this way. It was Mr Wilberforce himself who had sent Jim on that errand. Why? For what purpose? For his suicide? Jim had always looked after the old man during these evening bathes of his. Now, for the very first time—

The inspector was speaking again.

"Was this night swimming a habit of this guest of yours?"

"Oh yes, Mr Vincent. He bathe every night. With Jim's help. Jim carry the rubber mattress for him—"

"What rubber mattress?"

"He lay on it. Pushed himself about the pool. To avoid effort. He was an old man, Mr Vincent."

The inspector frowned. Another unusual feature in this case. A rubber mattress. Inflated, of course.

"Jim helped him," Mancini repeated. "Jim blew it up, helped him on to it, I think. You ask Jim."

"Where is the mattress now?"

Mancini waved his hands helplessly.

"You ask Jim," he repeated. "Jim know, I expect."

But the old gardener, who had sidled closer while the two were talking, now tugged at Mancini's sleeve.

"Looky here, man," he said, in a low voice. "Him down in water. Him rubber bed all right, all right. Down here. You looky down."

Chief-Inspector Vincent exclaimed, Mancini croaked in surprise and fear. Peering over the edge of the pool they saw it, a deflated, crumpled object, one end twisted under the side of the steps, which did not reach quite to the bottom of the pool.

Jim came running back with two bunched up sheets in his arms, followed at a distance by a more leisurely pair, the crew of the ambulance that had just driven up to the office of the hotel. Jim dropped to a walk as he reached the group at the pool, wincing as he was forced to see the still figure, its face now covered. He was passing the inspector and Mancini to complete his errand when the former stopped him.

"Look down in the water, Jim," Inspector Vincent ordered. "What do you see near the steps?"

"That Mas'r Wilb's lie-low. Name he called it. Lie-low."

"You carried it out here from his room last night when he came to bathe?"

"Not his room. That too wet. Always dry by kitchen porch. Therese see to it."

He backed away and the inspector let him go. Turning to his constable he said, "See if you can bring it out with the net. The old man will help you."

He had intended to watch this operation in order to see that the rubber mattress was not damaged during its recovery. But a cry of dismay, shock and terror breaking at that moment from Jim sent him spinning round in time to see the waiter fall on his knees beside the corpse. The ambulance men had stripped off the covering dressing gown and towel to replace them with one of the sheets, while the other, folded neatly, now lay on their stretcher waiting to receive the dead man. Jim's cry had frozen them where they stood. They held the sheet between them spread out. They now took a nervous step back, waiting.

"What's the matter?" asked Inspector Vincent, sharply. "Get up, man. Get up!"

"Is not Mas'r Wilb!" moaned Jim, rolling his eyes, clasping his hands. "Them feet, that body. Mas'r Wilb old man, very thin, white, *old*!"

The inspector felt a chill at the pit of his stomach. His profession, his training, his contact with modern police methods, with scientists in the forensic department at the university, his natural keen intelligence, all this had laid a hard cover over the seething superstitions of his race. Under the stress of this ghastly appearance, a young man's body, spare but muscular, well-built, brown, set below an old man's head, face and neck, closed eyelids, sparse grey hair, grey wrinkled skin, thin lips closed tightly. Closed—!

Inspector Vincent pulled himself together. He got down on his own knees beside Jim, pushing the latter back. He was a good Methodist, taught in a mission school. He spoke a short prayer inwardly to calm his fear. Behind him Mr Mancini crossed himself vigorously. The inspector passed his reluctant hand over the death mask; a true mask, he reassured himself, as he discovered no openings in that grim countenance. His hands moved mechanically as his spirit revived. He found the fastening at the back of the mask, hidden in the hair, he pulled off the old man's false head and face to disclose another, more in keeping with the body, quite surely attached to it, pale, with lips drawn back from gleaming teeth, dead but real.

Mr Mancini was staring at the mask in the inspector's hand. "It is Mr Wilberforce," he gasped. "It is a perfect likeness. I never saw it in his room. I never knew—"

"Never mind about your Mr Wilberforce," said Inspector Vincent roughly. "This man. Have you ever seen him before?"

"No," answered Mancini, who had turned his back on the corpse.

The two ambulance men, being used to strange unpleasant sights, had been only mildly shocked by the nasty joke played on this drowned young man. They were now covering him with the sheet they held, but stopped at an order from Vincent.

"But *you* know him?" he said to Jim, who had scrambled up from his knees, his face working with relief, bewilderment and a mounting joy. "You're *sure*. I can see it. Look again."

Jim looked and swallowed and turned away.

"Sure," he said firmly. "This man come two morning ago to see Mas'r Wilb. Show him to Paula. She know. She speak with him. She tell me take him to Mas'r Wilb. Mas'r Wilb not pleased. I think they have row. He go, this man. No car. Walking. Wanted money, maybe."

"All right, all right," Inspector Vincent was impatient. He had had a severe fright and he resented it. "I don't want your thoughts. I want facts. His name, for instance."

He had no hope of getting this and was astonished when Jim said very gravely, "Yes, sah. The name was Man— Manfrey Shine. Mas'r Wilb tell me I must remember this name. Man-frey Shine. From Venezuela. I think German, perhaps. Come on ship. German."

CHAPTER FIVE

At police headquarters in the city Inspector Vincent made his report to his superintendent. It was in many ways an unusual report, even startling. The police of Princeton were used to a certain amount of violence, occurring daily among a people of very mixed races, largely emotional, largely from countries European, Asian and African where a generous, indulgent sun nursed their impulses and their idleness.

But the grim circumstances of a youngish man's death at the run-down Gardenia Lodge Hotel did not fit the usual pattern at all. The superintendent of the uniformed side sent for his opposite number in the CID branch, a keen-faced, experienced West Indian, trained like Inspector Vincent by the colonial power. Detective-Superintendent Graham, given a brief summary of the finding of the body, sat down to listen while the uniformed superintendent left the room to go about his normal business.

"I found this occurrence strange from the beginning," Inspector Vincent explained to the newcomer. "The body, as the super told you—"

"Was seen by the gardener," interrupted Graham, not wishing to start again at the beginning.

"Was seen *floating* by the gardener," persisted Vincent, making the first point in his careful exposition. "Floating," he repeated, "as I myself saw also. But—" he forestalled another interruption with an upraised hand, "but sir, the rubber mattress had *sunk*."

"So?" asked the superintendent.

"So I ask myself two things," said Vincent, smugly. "Did the mattress sink under the victim, leaving him in the water to drown? Or was he dead, if or when he was placed on the mattress? Could this not so very young, but strong looking white man not swim? Or was he perhaps simply put, dead, into the water and the mattress sunk to hide it maybe for the time being?"

"Those are four things, not two, you ask," said Superintendent Graham, smiling, for he liked Vincent and admired his detective enthusiasm. "Four. And I add another. Was the mask fitted before the victim's death, before he was put in the water? It has no openings for nose or mouth. It would give suffocation."

He touched the mask that lay now on the table between them, its very natural features turned up to the ceiling, the closed eyelids, the closed mouth, the deep-lined grey skin presenting an inscrutable but powerfully unpleasant suggestion of strength and hidden knowledge.

"There was no sign of this," Vincent answered at once. "The man's face was pale, not congested. Besides, his hands and arms were free. He could have torn off the mask."

"Not if he was unconscious at the time," said the superintendent still staring at the mask of Mr Wilberforce as if to learn the answer from those fixed, thin lips.

"We must wait for the report from the hospital," he went on presently, as Inspector Vincent did not offer any more theories as to how the man had met his end. "In the meantime there is the interesting matter of his identity. Tell me again exactly what the waiter, Jim Hulbert, told you."

Vincent repeated this part of his report. Graham nodded.

"I have previous knowledge of this," he said. "He came from Venezuela on a Brazilian cargo vessel, arriving two days ago. He was listed as a member of the crew, giving the name of Manuela Garcia. He had papers in this name. He had served on this ship off and on for a number of years. They trade among many of the islands."

"When he came to the hotel he gave his name as George Wilberforce. He claimed to be the old man's nephew. The son of his brother, George Wilberforce. But Mr Wilberforce denied this relationship. He said the man was no relation. That his name was Manfry Shine."

"Which I take to be Manfred Stein," said the superintendent triumphantly. "Son of a well-known Nazi refugee in Venezuela, now dead, they tell me. The son joined his father when he was hounded out of Germany in his turn. They have both been on the run in South America for years, I understand."

Inspector Vincent was astonished. The detective-super had evidently been in touch with Security at a very high level to have learned all these particulars. It gave his case an added importance that was encouraging. All the same it did not seem to lead anywhere. Except for one fact.

"Why has this old man, this Mr Wilberforce, disappeared?" he asked, looking eagerly at Superintendent Graham.

The latter smiled.

"That is now your assignment, Inspector Vincent, if I can get you seconded to my side of things," he said blandly. "Go back to this Gardenia Lodge Hotel and discover all you can about him, including his present whereabouts. Report to me here this evening."

"Sir," said Inspector Vincent, his eyes shining with excitement. "I have no plain clothes here. I go home first?"

"No, no," Graham answered. "I haven't got it fixed with your super yet. Stick to your uniform. They know you in it up at the hotel. Might upset them if you turned up in anything else."

"Sir," Vincent repeated, on his feet now, with a very British salute learned in his early training in the force and never forgotten.

Meanwhile the dead man was conveyed to the University Hospital, where an immediate post-mortem examination was performed on the body.

This confirmed Inspector Vincent's theory that he had not drowned. There were no obvious marks of violence to be seen at first, no bullet holes or knife wounds. No gross outer violence at all. But it did not take long for the pathologist to discover that the man's neck had been broken by a skilled professional hand. He must have died at once. The gruesome details of his disposal, mask, swimming pool, rubber mattress and all, must have followed afterwards. There were no clues to suggest the slayer, nor whether death had taken the victim unaware or in the course of a desperate fight for his life.

"Except the mask," suggested Superintendent Graham, who had watched the post-mortem examination. "You understand that this Mr Wilberforce has not yet been located."

The pathologist looked very grave.

"You mean he might be the murderer?"

"That, or the murderer may have removed him too, putting his likeness on the first victim as a message, perhaps, or perhaps as a warning."

"Not a very nice thought," said the pathologist, who was an American and still felt a slight embarrassment in dealing with the coloured high officials in this island. "Who the heck would want to croak this guy, anyway?"

"Many people," answered Graham. He went on to explain who the man was, that he had landed with false papers, giving a fake name, as a seaman going ashore for a few hours before rejoining his ship. He had not rejoined. The master had reported this before sailing.

Superintendent Graham watched the pathologist's reaction to this piece of information, which was what he intended to release to the newspapers. It might be, he thought privately, that the man had intended to rejoin his ship if he had succeeded in whatever he came to Mr Wilberforce to get, which was most probably money. He had only Jim's word for what happened and the waiter had not been actually on the scene, though hovering nearby. However, Vincent was sure the man was reliable. He believed the stranger had tried to get money from Mr Wilberforce and failed. Perhaps he had come back to try again. Perhaps Mr Wilberforce was ready for him. Perhaps *that* was why the old man had very prudently disappeared. Leaving this horrible thing as a souvenir of his success?

Not a nice thought. And not at all consistent with all that was known in Security about Mr, formerly Colonel, Wilberforce.

He was no further towards a solution and he knew it. He looked at the pathologist and at the mortuary attendant, who had listened eagerly to all that had been said and was waiting now for the expected revelation; the full police explanation.

Graham smiled ironically. He had none yet to give; no satisfaction for the scientific intellect or the eager hunter of spells and their consequences. He said, briskly, "Well, Doctor, you will make out your report for me without delay, I hope." A thought came to him. "It would assist me and the inquest inquiry to have an X-ray confirmation of that broken neck. No need to make an elaborate dissection. Can you please arrange that?"

"Certainly," the pathologist answered. "I'll get hold of Dr Stone straight away."

For the superintendent the penny dropped just as his car was moving out of the hospital grounds. He told his driver to turn round and go back at once.

He was in time. A portable X-ray van was drawing up outside the mortuary. Two men stepped out of it. Graham followed.

Inside the building the pathologist stepped forward to greet his colleague. He noticed with surprise that the Law was back, moving in just behind the radiologist.

"Sorry to bother you, Stone," the pathologist said. "It's a case of probable mayhem. Someone's done a neat job of karate, looks like. Police want confirmation."

He stood aside, revealing the body and Dr Stone stepped forward.

He reacted immediately, violently. His face whitened, he spun round, taking in the circle of watching faces, which included now his own two assistants, carrying apparatus.

"This is a trap!" he cried, in a choking, guttural voice. "A dirty trap!"

Superintendent Graham, highly gratified by his own cleverness, said smoothly, "You recognise the deceased, then, Dr Stein? I should say, Dr Stone."

The pathologist was amazed. Stone was American, like himself. Of course he was of German extraction. That had always been clear from the way he spoke. Why not? His own forebears had been Dutch, but he never gave it a thought. Why should he? He was American. As for the name—

"I do not wish to interrupt the examination," Superintendent Graham said, watching the radiologist's efforts to control himself. "I will wait outside. Perhaps, Dr Stone, you will be good enough to see me when you have finished here."

"I'll see you in hell," said the radiologist, furiously.

"Then it will have to be at my office," answered Graham, his white teeth showing in a wide, genial grin that made his several compatriots present double up in silent laughter.

The superintendent waited in his car outside the mortuary. Dr Stone, advised and soothed by the pathologist, came stiffly to him there.

"We can speak in *your* office if you prefer," said the superintendent, politely. "Medical reason. No publicity."

"I have nothing to say to you anywhere," answered Dr Stone.

"Then we had better go to my office after all," said Graham. "You may decide different after a nice drive."

Dr Stone glared at the smooth black face and calm brown eyes, but he got into the back of the police car beside the superintendent and was driven away.

At the Gardenia Lodge Hotel Inspector Vincent found a very subdued staff and a very voluble proprietor.

Mr Mancini was distracted, but at the same time relieved. His early fears about the too-sudden death of the man whose life he had insured were now allayed. On the other hand, Mr Wilberforce had not been found, dead or dying or even totally unharmed. Mancini, as he explained to his wife, could bear to hear of a second murder, provided it had not taken place at or near the pool. What he could not bear was the suspense, the unendurable waiting, to hear of Mr Wilberforce's fate.

"He must be dead—but where?" he cried distractedly, over and over again. Until Maria, exasperated, said, "As if I could tell you! Have you gone out of your mind? To ask me—*me*—this silly question! Ask those policemen. By now they may know."

"They have gone away," he answered, equally exasperated by her lack of sympathy. "So how can I ask them?"

This conversation, repeated in essence and in more and more unseemly words as the hours passed, continued until the afternoon when Maria, looking out between the curtains of their darkened room, said, "Ask those policemen. Ask them now. They have just gone into the office."

Grumbling at the interruption of his siesta Mancini hurried into a singlet and trousers and went out into the drive, while Maria returned to the bed, pulled the sheet over her and slept.

Inspector Vincent received the flood of Mancini's pent-up impatience. He had come to question the hotel owner and staff, but for a time this was not possible. Mancini asked the questions with too much rapid insistence. However, the inspector had very little to tell him and managed to make it plain that even if he knew the answers he was not going to give them. In the end he simply turned his broad back on the still chattering proprietor and spoke to Paula.

She confirmed what he already knew about the German's arrival the day before.

"Then there was the other George Wilberforce," she said. "The American one."

Inspector Vincent had not heard of this before.

"He came in a car," the girl said, "to see his uncle Mr Wilberforce. I think it very strange, two nephews the same day. Then I remember the two telegrams, both coming the day before this and the letter before that."

"*Two* telegrams? Both in the same name?"

"That so. Both signed George. The letter was by airmail, sent by Mrs Lucy Maclean. It gave name and address in England on the back. You ask Jim. Mr Wilberforce tell Jim things. Not me."

"You don't live here, do you, Miss?"

"I do not," she answered, with a glint in her large dark eyes.

Inspector Vincent left the office, half expecting to be pounced on again by Mr Mancini. But the drive was empty, except for the police car with the driver reading a newspaper and nearby a big Ford Cortina that had arrived during the last few minutes. It was empty, but he noticed several young men and a girl sitting in the shadows of the deep verandah that ran along in front of the doors of the guest rooms in the block at the head of the drive. They were murmuring together in low voices. They had suitcases beside them.

Were they incoming or outgoing guests of this busy place, the inspector wondered, ironically. He stood still in the middle of the drive, considering. The group continued to chatter, not looking his way; the thin cat came from the bushes and stood still also, regarding him, its tail moving slowly from side to side. A lizard froze with spread legs just in front of his foot. He lifted the foot over it and went on towards a door with dustbins beside it. He knocked and waited.

The door was opened at once by Therese, who called to Jim before the inspector had time to explain himself.

The waiter was not far off. He came at once, as eager as his master to hear the latest news, but prepared for reticence and not resentful when he was told nothing.

"I couldn't get a word in edgeways with your boss," Vincent began, "so I hope you can help me. How long have you been here, for a start? In old man Stewart's time?"

"Man, he give me my first job," answered Jim, heartily. "He was good man. Gardenia good place those days, you know. Six waiters. Five days all meals served out on the loggia by the pool—"

Vincent stopped him, not unkindly.

"I know. I know. It is not the same. It will never be the same. Look at all those fine new factories outside in the road. A little quiet hotel, how can it attract now?"

Jim shook his head. There was no answer. Gardenia had been swallowed up, by independence and by the factories.

"Now," said the inspector briskly. "Last night. Tell me again exactly what happened."

The waiter repeated his story, carefully, truthfully, up to his return to the hotel after delivering the letter.

"You then went at once to bed, assuming Mr Wilberforce was back in his room?"

"Thass right, sah."

"I am surprised you didn't make sure by going up to the pool to see he was not there."

"He tole me he was going to manage. He tole me take the letter and he would manage."

Inspector Vincent suspected this was not the whole story but saw he would not shake Jim just yet.

"When you went to the pool with Mr Wilberforce what exactly happened? Tell me again."

"We went to pool. Mas'r Wilb took his towel to put in little house. Then he come out quickly, catch my arm so I drop the mattress, begin to push me back along pool. He'd remember, you know sah, very important message for lawyer, Mr Gopal. He very angry he forget. Feared Mr Gopal not at home, maybe."

"Yes." Inspector Vincent had heard this before in much the same words. It was all probably true, except that piece about going to bed at once.

"When you got back," he asked again. "Did you try to tell Mr Wilberforce you had been successful in delivering the letter? Did you go to see if there was a light in his room?"

"No light," said Jim, truthfully, seeing also that this was a way out. "No light. No use to disturb."

Inspector Vincent, watching as he made some show of writing in his notebook, saw Jim glance anxiously at his wife, who stood beside him, resting her large bulk against the stout wooden kitchen table. He said, without looking up, "About this mask. Not a nice thing to have, was it? Did he ever tell you why he had it, where it was made, when it was made?"

"Never tell me anything," Jim said violently, beginning to shiver. "Never see it till today. Think—in the water, I think—"

"You thought it was Mr Wilberforce," said the inspector calmly. "So did I. So did Mr Mancini. So did everyone else, until we took it off."

"They think so still," whispered Jim. "The girls, Paula, when they tell her, that garden man, Therese my wife here."

"Not Therese," that lady replied, heaving herself away from the table as she spoke. "Mr Police, I knew from one, two months back. I knew."

"How?" Inspector Vincent's voice was sharper now. He had heard the fear in Jim's voice, seen it in his trembling hands. The old fear, born in him, nourished by grandparents, by his mother, until his training began to blot it out. If Therese could clear away the rising clinging grey cobweb of fear from the bottom of his own mind she could do the same for the others in this poor stricken house.

"How?" he repeated, fixing his eyes on her, demanding the real, factual, commonsense truth.

"Doan know how long he got it," Therese said, beginning to regret her confession. "I never like to ask him. It were one day I thought to ask him if I put achee in his rice, or too hot for him? I look in at window—he there on bed lying down asleep. As I think. I hear someone in corridor and stay in corner, waiting. Mr Wilberforce go past me. He say, 'Therese, wot the matter? You ill?' and I say, 'Ill with fright, Mas'r Wilb. You here and you in there, asleep. One of you'se spirit. Not know which.' I kneel down with fright, you understand. I ask help to Jesus. My knees go soft to think he really houngan or even zombie and we not know at all."

"Then what happened?" asked Inspector Vincent, fascinated by this unexpected tale.

"He laugh," Therese said, with disgust. "Pull me up and take me in his room. Pull the sheet off the bed and there was two pillows endways and at top this thing fastened on lump of wood. He say I must never speak of it to any living soul. I never did till now. Because he gone and I think he dead and does not hear."

Her eyes filled with tears, which spilled down her cheeks as Jim reached out to take her hand.

Inspector Vincent turned to go. He had learned enough already to turn in something fresh to Superintendent Graham. But he had an appointment with the old man's lawyer, Henry Gopal. Jim had confirmed that the letter sent by Wilberforce had been delivered safely. There was more, much more, he needed to know about the vanished man's affairs, his past and his presence in San Fernando. He suspected that Superintendent Graham already knew something of this. It would do no harm to check for himself, since the Super had not taken him into his confidence.

As Vincent went back to his car in the drive a taxi drew up near it and a white girl got out. While the taxi driver lifted down a suitcase from the seat beside him the girl went into the office. Inspector Vincent heard her say to Paula, in a clear English accent, "Good afternoon. I telephoned you this morning from the harbour to reserve a room. I am Alison Maclean. My uncle, Mr Benedict Wilberforce, is staying with you, I believe."

CHAPTER SIX

Inspector Vincent was torn between his wish to report his discovery about the mask and the fresh urge to interview the vanished man's niece. He stood by his car for a few minutes, considering. But when he saw the taxi leave and Paula come out of the office to call for Jim; when he saw the pale face of the newcomer, bewildered, apprehensive, emerge behind her, he stepped into the police car, ordering his driver to take him back to headquarters.

It would be useless to start on the girl now, he decided. She would have nothing to tell. He could report her arrival and by the time Superintendent Graham had made up his mind how to deal with her presence at the hotel, the girl would have grasped the situation and would, if she were not involved in it, be prepared to help the police to the best of her ability.

Superintendent Graham was not altogether pleased by this new development, of which he had not been warned. It added a fresh black mark to Mancini's score. According to what Vincent had overheard the girl had made a reservation. Mancini must have known this. He might have forgotten to report it during the excitements and distresses of finding a dead man in his swimming pool, but afterwards when the body had been removed and with it his immediate responsibility, he should have mentioned the fact. It was directly connected with Mr Wilberforce. The girl had come expecting to see her uncle. He was no longer at the hotel. Her arrival was a strange coincidence; it needed further investigation. Also the contents of Mr Wilberforce's room, his papers and so on.

The room had been sealed. While Graham was at the mortuary the uniformed superintendent had looked after that. But neither he nor Superintendent Graham trusted the Mancinis. Graham looked at his watch.

"I have to see this man, Gopal, that Jim told us he'd taken a letter to. Indian lawyer, I understand."

He made a face of disgust, with which Vincent was in complete sympathy.

"I'm due there now. I'd like you to go back to Gardenia Lodge. Talk to this girl, put her in the picture and find out all you can about her background in England, when she last saw her uncle, where he was living, there or in some other country. He's been in San Fernando a little over a year, apparently. Security have a file on him. That's as far as I've got with them."

He shuffled the papers on his desk, distractedly. Too much to tie up, too much to do. All on account of a miserable ex-Nazi, son of a Nazi, who'd got what was coming to him. Why here, why not in Venezuela? Why did he have to get himself killed at Mancini's of all places? Why involve Wilberforce? Where was the old boy, anyhow? Dr Stone was a distant cousin of the dead man, so he'd said, but denied having anything to do with him, his whereabouts, his actions, his curious link with Wilberforce. Lies? Very likely.

Vincent watched the superintendent, waiting for him to finish his orders or to show that he had finished.

"Well, get going!" Graham shouted, overcome by the formidable size of his problem.

"Sir," Vincent said, stung out of lethargy. He saluted, turned on his heel and hurried away.

Meanwhile Alison, quite ignorant of the fact that the police had observed her arrival, was both alarmed and incredulous at the news of her uncle's disappearance. She began to ask Paula for details, but the girl did not answer, only went outside into the drive, calling for Jim. After waiting a few minutes for the waiter, who did not arrive, she went back into the office, laid the hotel register before the newcomer and handed her a ballpoint pen.

After a moment's reflection Alison took it and filled in the necessary details. Uncle or no uncle, she must stay at least one night in this place, if only to find out where he was and why he had left, without leaving a note of explanation, knowing that she was due to arrive that day. Or did he not know? She asked Paula.

"Mr Wilberforce did ask me if you make a reservation," Paula answered, truthfully. "Two days, three days, I don't remember. I tell him no."

"I wrote for one," Alison said, indignantly. "The letter was posted in Trinidad three days ago. An airmail letter."

"I get no letter," Paula answered. But turning to a pile of unopened envelopes on her desk she picked out one and held it up.

"This maybe," she said, slitting it open. "Come by post this morning. But you hear of our trouble this morning."

"How could I hear anything?" Alison cried, impatiently. "I only left the ship this afternoon. I was trying for hours to get you on the phone."

"We have this trouble," Paula repeated, calmly.

She came from behind the counter, went to a board on the wall where keys hung on three rows of hooks and taking one from the board said, "I show you your room. Be not quite ready, but I show you."

She led the way across the drive to the verandah where the six young people were still sitting slumped in metal chairs, their legs sprawling in front of them. Paula picked her way between the legs and the suitcases of their owners, followed by Alison, who tried to suppress the indignation she felt at this display of what she considered flagrant bad manners.

Paula unlocked the door of the room and held it open for Alison to go in. Then she handed her the key and said, "I now find Jim to bring your luggage. Lizzie will come, too, with sheets."

Left to herself Alison put down her smaller suitcase which she had carried from the office and laid her handbag on the wide dressing table. The room was evidently a double one, with a spacious bed, a large hanging cupboard and small drawers on either side of the knee-hole dressing table. On one side of the wide looking glass stood a telephone, on the other a bible in English, provided by the society that furnishes hotels everywhere with the word of God.

At the far end of the room another door stood ajar. Alison pushed it open and found herself in her bathroom. In keeping with all she had seen of the hotel so far, the paint here too was peeling, the lavatory seat needed a screw and wobbled, the wash-basin was cracked, as was the mirror over it.

But the bath was magnificent, long, wide, deep, tiled in a deep red and orange stippled pattern, with a shower and curtains, but only one tap that ran cold. Both the wash-basin taps ran cold.

This did not trouble her; she welcomed it. Though she enjoyed heat and sunshine, her day so far had been very strenuous and after twelve days at sea spent chiefly, after leaving the Azores, in the ship's bathing pool or lying in the sun, she found the harbour berth unbearably hot and the drive through the town stifling. As soon as her luggage arrived and her room was properly prepared she promised herself a long, cool shower. In the meantime she turned up the air conditioning to maximum cold and sat on the edge of the bed as near it as possible, to wait.

After half an hour she became tired of waiting. She went to her door and opened it, deciding to search the verandah and the other hotel rooms for Lizzie, who was supposed to be making her bed and bringing towels.

The six visitors with their suitcases and soft holdalls were still there, blocking her way. Twelve dark eyes turned towards her, six sprawling figures shifted a little in her direction, six dark faces grew blank and still. Alison said, "I wonder if you can tell me where to find Lizzie?" There was no answer, no movement, no change of expression, no response whatsoever.

Alison stared back at the six, her father's Scottish blood suddenly roused. Her mother was never tired of telling her how much she resembled her father, both in character and in appearance. But in her his flaming red hair was reduced to a rich chestnut, his light blue eyes changed to violet, fringed with black eyelashes and framed by black eyebrows, his freckled skin replaced by a smooth unblemished cream colour unchanged by the sun that had tanned her arms and legs. She was tall and slender, very upright, standing in her doorway staring, the light of cold anger shining in the violet eyes. Just like her father, her mother would have said.

"Perhaps none of you can tell me," she said softly, in the clear, fighting Scots voice and accent that had so often reduced her schoolmates to panic.

The six black visitors stirred. The one directly outside her door, whose bag lay in her path, pulled himself up a little, stretched out a long, sensitive hand, tweaked the obstruction a little closer to him. Alison stepped past it, turned, locked her door, began to move away.

A girl in a very short mini-skirt, sitting opposite the man who had moved, said, "You want Lizzie, mistress? We wants Lizzie too. That Paula say she do our rooms. Not done."

"Then we're all in the same boat," Alison said, restored, smiling. "I'll see if I can find her."

She went back to the office. Paula was not there, her suitcase stood where the taxi driver had placed it. Paula's second in command seemed not to understand a word Alison spoke. Her anger rising again, she left the office, went across the drive and down the corridor. She walked through the dining room and the darkened lounge and out on to the lounge verandah. She found Jim there, talking to the old gardener.

Jim at once took charge of the situation. He had not been told of her arrival, he said. To her first question about her uncle he answered, "Long story, Mistress Mac—Mac—"

"Miss Maclean. Mr Wilberforce's niece. His sister's daughter."

Jim's face brightened with understanding.

"He tell me he expect you. From England. So bad he not here. You take drink? What you like?"

"Anything cold," Alison said. "Lots of ice. Any kind of fruit juice. Orange, pineapple—"

"I get that," Jim said. "Then I tell you."

He was back in no time, with a long glass frosted by the ice in it, two straws and a little plate of almonds. Propping himself against one of the pillars of the verandah, he told her what had happened. He told her about the visits of the two nephews and what had happened to one of them.

"But what's become of Uncle Ben?" Alison demanded, her confusion and distress making her voice rise. "Does no one know where he is?"

"The police maybe. We not know here. I think he will send message. I hope."

"You know him well, don't you?" Alison asked, urgently. "You're his friend?"

Jim nodded. She watched the dark face grow soft, the eyes fill with tears. Poor old Jim, she thought, he's rather a pet and he does think a lot of Uncle Ben. She felt she could trust Jim.

She said so. She added, "Will you help me to find him? And tell me how to send a telegram to my mother."

For answer Jim went away and came back with the late edition of the island's principal evening newspaper. He showed her the Press release in a paragraph on the front page. When she had read it she looked up again at Jim.

"It's just as you told me," she said. "They think they know who the man was who was found here in the pool. A German, apparently. It says very little, though. Of course he wasn't my uncle's nephew. You do realise that, don't you?"

"But it says Mas'r Wilb gone away, not know where. This news will go to England, I think. Your mother, Mistress Maclean, will read it. Soon as telegram. Not cost anything."

Alison laughed. She finished her drink, got to her feet.

"Please help me with my suitcase," she said, smiling. "And then tell me where to find this Mr Gopal. I must see him today if possible. But I must get properly fixed up in my room, first."

"That Lizzie!" Jim exclaimed.

After this, Alison's problems were resolved in a very short time. Jim shouted to Therese in the kitchen as he passed it on the way back to the office. Therese could be heard shouting in her turn. By the time Jim had picked up the suitcase and carried it across the drive, Alison following, the six arrivals who had settled round her door had disappeared. In spite of their luggage, which she had seen, and their air of possession, which she had unreasonably found offensive, she never saw them again, either on the verandah, at meals, or in the public rooms of the hotel. Jim told her later that they were still there, but went out early and came back late. Well, there was nothing criminal in that, though she found it vaguely disturbing, totally alien. This former small part of Britain was in reality a wholly foreign country, had perhaps, since the first mixing of races there, compelled or voluntary, always been so.

At the time of her return to her room she was simply relieved to find no bags or suitcases in her path and a short, plump, brown-faced girl waiting for the door to be unlocked.

"Is there no master key?" Alison asked, very conscious of having put her room key in her handbag when she went to find Jim.

The girl shook her head, not understanding the question. Jim also shook his head, not bothering to explain. Alison opened her door.

When Jim had gone away after putting down the large suitcase, the girl who now gave her name as the missing Lizzie, went away and returned with an armful of bed linen and towels. Alison, who was impatient for her long delayed shower, said briskly, "I'll help you make the bed, shall I?"

Lizzie giggled. She did not refuse the offer, but she went on giggling at intervals during the whole operation which, since it consisted simply of laying on two sheets, two pillow cases and a bedspread, with a folded wool blanket at the foot, took a few short minutes and scarcely any effort.

"What's the great joke?" Alison asked, smiling.

Lizzie managed to say, "You from England, mam? Mos' white folk from States now."

"Americans, you mean?"

"That so, mam. Speak different. Make me laugh hear that way you speak. English people not stay, not tourists."

This was true, Alison thought sadly. Of the other passengers on board her ship the majority were there for the round cruise, a few were landing to take up jobs at the university or in branches of British business firms, one or two, like herself, to visit relations, a few more, all coloured, to return to their homes in San Fernando. The only tourists she had known were some who had joined the ship at Trinidad.

So she nodded agreement with Lizzie and asked, "Do you have many American tourists staying here, Lizzie?"

The girl answered readily enough, "Three come today. I think business gentlemen, not tourists."

"Who else is staying here?"

"One lady, but she not tourist. Lives across mountains at Freeman's Bay. Very beautiful mountains. You tourist. Go visit."

"I came to visit my uncle," Alison said, rousing herself from the lethargy into which she had fallen. She turned out Lizzie, locked her door, unfastened her suitcase and hung up her dresses in the big wall cupboard. Then, sweating again from this fresh effort, she turned on the bath tap and stripping quickly was soon up to her ankles in cold water while a stream from the shower played over her body as she turned slowly round and round.

This delight, however, was brought to an end by a loud knocking on her door. Wrapping herself in a rather skimpy towel she went to it and called out, "Who's that?"

"Jim," the now familiar voice answered. "Missy Maclean, there's police officer to see you. Inspector Vincent. Please to open door."

"Certainly not," Alison answered. "I'm having a shower. Ask the inspector to wait. I'll be as quick as I can."

She heard a muttered conversation begin on the verandah, but did not wait to hear it. However, it took her very few minutes to get into a pair of pale green linen slacks and a loose sleeveless green and yellow cotton shirt. Pushing her feet into straw sandals she unlocked her door and looked outside. Her thick, auburn hair lay closely about her head and face, trimmed for the voyage to the tropics much shorter than she wore it at home. She had not waited to put on make-up. This

was a point in her favour with Inspector Vincent who rose
from his seat on the verandah as he saw her door open.

"Miss Alison Maclean?" he asked, politely.

The girl nodded and hesitated, then held out her hand. The
burly frame, the smart uniform, the intelligent dark eyes and
distinct speech promised more definite protection and clearer
understanding than any she had met since she landed. Jim,
however good-hearted, however loyal to her uncle, could not
help her as this man could. When his own hand came out to
meet hers she clasped it with sudden fervour before letting it
go.

Inspector Vincent, keenly aware of her state of confusion and
perhaps shock, was gratified by this mark of trust.

"I think we will speak in my car," he said. "Unless you will
find it too hot. There is nowhere in the hotel where we cannot
be overheard."

Alison was sure the police car would be blistering. It would
undo all the good work of her shower. But she went with the
inspector meekly until, seeing the swimming pool from the
drive, she exclaimed, "Surely no one can hear us from up
there if we speak quietly?"

"From beside the pool, do you mean?" Inspector Vincent was
astonished. Had she not been told—?

"Yes. Why not?"

"The—the incident—the discovery—"

"Oh, you mean that German who was drowned or killed or
something? He has nothing to do with me. Or has he? I mean
on account of Uncle Ben. Anyway, he isn't in the pool now.
So why—?"

Her calm indifference surprised the inspector anew. Granted
she was not plagued by superstition. But ordinary human feelings, feminine human feelings—

Alison saw his surprise, his disapproval.

"I'm not really being callous," she said. "It's just that people
in England still can't feel very cordial to Nazis. I was born in
the War, so I was too young to know then. But my mother and

father—so many of their friends—younger cousins—My crook uncle—"

She stopped speaking suddenly, looking sideways at Inspector Vincent as if to find out how much he had already heard of the family history.

"We will go to that bench at the shallow end of the pool," the inspector said. "Follow me."

He led the way across the shaded, neglected loggia, where the chairs and tables lay heaped together in confusion, past the wooden contraption that had been used in prosperous times as a bar, to the steps that led up to the pool and the metal seat beside it.

When they were seated Vincent went over the events of the last few days, including the disappearance of Colonel Wilberforce, as he called him. He mentioned the mask and was pleased to note the horror on the girl's face as he described its most recent use. So she was not altogether insensitive, in spite of her race, in spite of her strange colouring, which he found unattractive.

"It's all very mysterious," Alison said, when he fell silent. "I think the best thing I can do is to find that Mr Gopal that Jim took a letter to."

Damn Jim, thought the inspector, I left that out on purpose. Aloud he said, "The best thing you can do, Miss Maclean, is to fly back to England as soon as we can find you a place on a plane."

"Oh no," Alison answered. "I can't do that! Who—except you people, of course—would find Uncle Ben? He hasn't been well. I know that from a letter he wrote to my mother. He may need me. There's no one else."

"From tomorrow morning," Inspector Vincent said, annoyed by what he considered her self-importance, "there will be someone far more able than you to deal with this situation."

"What do you mean?" she asked breathlessly.

"Your mother, it appears, has been anxious about you. Why, we do not yet know. But we have been notified, only a few hours ago, that Mistress Maclean has persuaded her own lawyer, a Mr Grant—"

"*Not* the old man!" Alison interrupted, in dismay.

"You don't like—" Vincent began, but checked himself. "A Mr Peter Grant," he explained. "He is flying here overnight."

"*Peter!*" Alison's dismay, though now from a different cause, was unrelieved. The last time she had met Peter, at a rather boring party, they had quarrelled. It had been an occasion of test, as far as she was concerned. He had offered to drive her home if she wanted to leave early. She had told him she must wait for her mother, hoping he would insist upon taking her and suggest a new arrangement for her mother, who was as capable as she of driving the family car. He did not insist, so she did. The degree of emotion generated in this futile argument should have produced results, Alison decided, nursing her bruised feelings for the rest of that evening. Perhaps he would ring up and say—what? She waited and hoped. He did not ring up. Three days later she had joined the *Benito* at Southampton.

"This does not please you?" Inspector Vincent said, watching her.

"No. I mean yes. Of course, Peter will be able to find Uncle Ben. It's just that—"

"Yes?"

"Never mind. Something. Perhaps Mr Gopal can tell me."

Inspector Vincent rose to his feet, fixing his uniform cap on his short black curls.

"It will not be possible for you to see Mr Gopal today," he said firmly. "He is engaged with Detective-Superintendent Graham. And tomorrow you will be advised by Mr Peter Grant. So I will now say goodbye, Miss Maclean. May I ask that you will show that English patience we were taught to admire when I was a little boy."

Alison looked at him without rancour. He was not trying to needle her, he spoke sincerely and hopefully, which she found touching. But she could not resist saying, as she shook hands with him again, "But I'm a Scot, Inspector, or a half Scot, anyway. We have frightful tempers when we're roused and if I don't find Uncle Ben soon I'm afraid you'll find out it's true."

"Then we will find him soon," Inspector Vincent said calmly, unimpressed and walked away to his car.

CHAPTER SEVEN

Superintendent Graham's interview with Mr Gopal told him very little he did not already know, but at the same time it made him realise how little the island's Security branch had been able to give him. The fact was that Wilberforce had lived quietly in San Fernando, apparently a retired man with a half-buried past, and because he gave no trouble of any kind, Security had not bothered its head about him. Until now.

"He is a very unfortunate man," Mr Gopal explained. "He comes of a good family, soldiers of the officer class for several generations, which means during the building and consolidation of the late British Empire."

He allowed himself a discreet smile, which the superintendent did not reciprocate.

"He entered the British Army himself and reached the rank of colonel. He distinguished himself in the Second World War. Unfortunately his brother George was a crook, an ordinary unscrupulous reckless thief, embezzler, forger of cheques and documents, swindler—"

"But for a time successful, I am given to understand."

"Exactly. With his family connections—they were not all soldiers, some held government posts, some had successful businesses—he managed to keep his real vocation secret. He used many different names. His criminal associates never knew much about him. It is not an unusual story, except that he lasted so long before the crash came. Also he seems to have stashed away so much of his ill-gotten wealth so successfully."

"Have we any proof of this?"

"Not as far as I am concerned. But I do know that he served a stiff sentence in English prisons, managed to emigrate to the States with his wife, and his son who was born just before the crash and was about ten years old when he was released. How they managed to settle in America I do not know. But I do know they were not poor, not at first."

"Why do you say that?"

"Because it is known that they lived well on private means, said to be provided by the wife. She had lived quietly but comfortably during the prison years and gave the boy a good education. In the States they were more than comfortable, apart from the boy's, the young man's as he soon became, gross habits—gambling, women, drink. The old man died some years ago. Recently the son went to England and began plaguing his aunt. Writing to her. Asking for money. Blackmail, to all intents and purposes. This Colonel Wilberforce told me. He'd had a letter from her, warning him."

"Of what?"

"Of young George's intention to come here and extract money from his uncle."

Superintendent Graham stretched himself. They were taking an unholy time in getting to the point.

"It is about Colonel Wilberforce, as you call him," he began, but Mr Gopal interrupted.

"He *was* a colonel," he said. "He resigned his commission when his brother was convicted and sent to prison."

"Gave up his career voluntarily, eh?" Graham said, nodding. "We have wondered about that."

"It is true," Gopal insisted. "It was a very severe blow to him. His life was the Army. He had not married. All his friends were Army men. His superior officers were reluctant to let him go. But they saw that the scandal was too bad. You see George, the scoundrel, insisted that Benedict had taken a half share of the profits of his crimes throughout."

"Surely it could be proved that he had not?"

"Of course. He was never accused of being an accomplice. But mud sticks, doesn't it? The colonel had no idea his brother was crooked. He relied on him to make his occasional investments. This was, in fact, profitable until the smash. Benedict beggared himself giving back every penny he possessed. But, as I said, mud sticks, you know."

"So then what did your colonel do? He was still fairly young, wasn't he?"

"Fifty-three. They took him on as a security agent. South America. He knew Spanish. Also he'd been attached to an exploration team when he was quite young and spent over a year in the remoter parts of Brazil, the Amazon headwaters, too, I believe. This later job was political, not geographical. Part of it was tracing escaped, prominent ex-Nazis. The rest was locating communist guerilla cells in British colonies and their neighbouring states."

Mr Gopal ceased speaking, but as the superintendent waited, still looking expectant, he said, irritably, "That's all I know of his past. You must have his record in San Fernando. You must have a file on him, haven't you?"

"Yah, yah, we have a file." Graham sat forward. "To come to the present. You have seen him the day before he disappeared. The day before the body of the Nazi, Manfred Stein, was found at his hotel."

"Two days before Stein was found. The day Stein paid him a visit, tried to pretend he was his nephew, young George. That day Colonel Wilberforce came to make a new will. In the late afternoon when he had seen the real George Wilberforce. So he told me."

He explained the old man's story of two telegrams, two interviews, two refusals.

"The story of hidden treasure again," Graham said, thoughtfully. "It sticks, doesn't it?"

"You must ask young George."

"If we find him. No one has come to San Fernando in that name. No one presented a passport in that name on the day these two men came to see Wilberforce. Nor on any other day. Stein's false passport we know about. Not the other."

"Then you will have to check all recent incoming Americans. The colonel told me he looked and spoke like an American. He had lived in the States since before he was ten, as I told you. I believe his mother had American connections. Probably that helped her to get in with the boy."

The superintendent nodded.

"This new will—" he began, but the lawyer interrupted him.

"Was ready for signature as and when he asked me. I have had my instructions. I can tell you nothing about them. I will carry them out as given. There has been unexpected delay but I do as I am asked."

"Was there nothing in that letter he sent down by the hotel waiter the night he left the place? Went without anyone's knowledge, apparently. Taking any papers he had by him, if any, but leaving a big holdall of clothes."

"Is that so?" said Mr Gopal, politely. If this was unexpected, he gave no sign of it.

"Where is he?" Superintendent Graham demanded suddenly, rising to his full height, a commanding, even threatening figure. "Where is he and where is that letter he sent by Jim?"

"The letter is in my safe, where it will remain," said Mr Gopal, rising in his turn. He was a full eight inches shorter than the detective, but his dignity and self-assurance gave him added stature.

"As I have told you he sent me his instructions and I follow them. He has enemies, that is obvious. He may well have decided to hide from them for a time. He is a sick man. He may have become worse, even died. He may have been kidnapped, killed, possibly."

"He may have killed Manfred Stein," said Graham. "The

mask was his. It was perhaps used as a hallmark of his crime."

Mr Gopal smiled coldly.

"That," he said, "is the most unlikely thing you have said to me."

Superintendent Graham controlled his instant rage with an effort. He hesitated, then sat down again. Mr Gopal considered this as gross impertinence, but said nothing and slowly resumed his own seat.

"I take it you want to assist me?" Graham said gruffly. "Is it because you are hiding something or because you know very little about Mr Wilberforce?"

As the lawyer made no answer, he went on, "Mr Wilberforce has private means, I take it? He is not employed any longer by the British. Was there a pension?"

"There was a pension," answered Gopal, seeing that he could not avoid these questions. "It would cease at his death. He had, also, a plantation, a coffee plantation, in this island. It was on account of the plantation that he came here a year ago and stayed here. He bought the plantation some years ago, while on leave from his work in South America."

The superintendent sat on in silence for a few seconds, thinking over this unexpected information. Security had said nothing of any plantation.

"Coffee," he muttered at last. "A few years ago. He'd get his plantation cheap, then. They were all turning over to bananas or cane at that time. Or even onions."

"So he told me," said Mr Gopal, primly. "He preferred coffee. Especially since it is such very excellent coffee."

"He makes a bit out of it, does he?"

"I think so. Enough to make it worth while to keep it in production."

"Ah." The superintendent paused, then he said, "You will give me the address of this plantation, please."

Mr Gopal opened his hands apologetically.

"I am sorry. I have no exact address. Somewhere in the Barrack Hill area of the mountains. That is all I know."

Superintendent Graham rose again, this time with the firm intention of leaving. Gopal might be speaking the truth or he might not, but he would give nothing more away. On the other hand it was quite possible that the old man, Wilberforce, had gone into hiding on his plantation, if he were free and still alive. Particularly if he had murdered the German. Searching the mountains for an unnamed, near obsolete coffee patch was not an inviting prospect. Something, perhaps, he could shift on to Inspector Vincent's uniformed shoulders.

He thanked the lawyer gravely for his help and moved to the door of the office.

"If you hear from Colonel Wilberforce you will tell me at once," he said. It was not a request, it was an order.

"If the colonel gets in touch with me I will advise him to contact you at once," answered Gopal.

It was by no means the same thing, the superintendent thought as he went out into the glare of the street. But these Indians were a slippery lot. Got so many of the good jobs, too. Education. That was the clue. In time his own people would get the good jobs. In time. He told his driver to take him to the University Hospital.

Dr Grigg was making a ward round when the superintendent appeared. The latter was shown into the ward sister's room, where a nurse came in almost at once with a cup of coffee. Perhaps Wilberforce's coffee, he thought, stirring it idly. But when he sipped the first mouthful he nearly spat it out in disgust. It was only coffee essence, the sort of thing American tourists carried about in tins, asking for hot water to make their nauseous brew.

Dr Grigg did not keep him waiting long. He appeared, calmly efficient, cool in his long white coat. He accepted a steaming cup from the same little nurse who had supplied the superintendent and who now took away the nearly full cup he pushed towards her.

Superintendent Graham explained his position.

"Your patient has vanished, Doctor," he said. "I would like

to know, if you can tell me, exactly what his physical condition is worth."

"Very little," said Dr Grigg cheerfully. "I warned him only a day or two ago. Admittedly he was upset on that day— family trouble, I believe. But the latest X-ray—"

"Can you explain that, Doctor."

Dr Grigg was put out. He frowned, hesitated, turned to his houseman, a young Chinese from San Francisco with a round, intelligent face.

"Can you find Dr Faulkner for me, Chen?" he said, looking at his watch. "Ask him to slip up here if he will. And get hold of the notes of Colonel Benedict Wilberforce. Heart case. I saw him a couple of days ago. They'll help you in Records. But get hold of Dr Faulkner first, please."

"O.K. Dr Gligg."

The doctor watched him go, then turned to Graham again.

"I'm sorry, but this is my last day here and as you can imagine I'm absolutely up to the eyes, signing off in every sense of the word. But I've sent for my successor, Dr Faulkner. He takes over as from the end of this morning. He knows the hospital well. He has been a registrar here for six months. Now he starts a year as medical consultant."

All very interesting, the superintendent thought, but not relevant to the case of Wilberforce. He said nothing, however, and before many minutes had passed Chen came back carrying a bulky file and following a tall young man considerably younger than Dr Grigg. He was introduced as Dr Brian Faulkner from London.

Dr Faulkner said pleasantly that he thought he remembered the old chap as he had seen him when Dr Grigg was on holiday the previous Christmas. The latter excused himself and went away. Superintendent Graham explained his needs all over again to the newcomer.

"It's a question of Colonel Wilberforce's physical condition, you see," he said, when he had described the dead man's injury and the finding of the body. "Would this elderly man be physically capable of the killing and the disposal in this manner?"

"Why should he want to kill him?" asked Dr Faulkner reasonably.

"That is too complicated to go into and besides it would not be desirable to discuss it. There was what could be called a motive."

"You surprise me. He seemed a very peaceable old man the only time I saw him."

During these exchanges Dr Faulkner had been turning over the notes in the file. Two large envelopes, attached to these notes, held X-ray negatives, which he now drew out and held up to the light.

"Dr Grigg mentioned the X-rays," Graham said.

"Quite. I don't quite understand—" Dr Faulkner began again at the beginning of the series, exclaimed aloud, referred once more to the notes, then pushed them from him.

"Got a viewing box in the ward, Sister?" he asked, turning to the nurse who had watched the whole proceeding with interest.

"Of course, sir. This way."

"You come, too," Faulkner said, turning to Graham. "Bring the notes along, Chen."

Superintendent Graham listened and watched. It was not difficult and very interesting.

"You see," the doctor explained after running through the whole series. "The heart enlargement remains moderate throughout. But in the last two films there is a fresh development—you see this shadow to the left of the upper part of the heart. Now the last picture taken just a fortnight ago. Gross change."

He explained the nature of an aneurysm, the bulging and thinning, in this case the big artery leading away from the heart. He explained the dangers, in this case a very acute danger.

"I wouldn't give him more than a couple of months on that

evidence," he said. "I would say that if he did the things you suspect him of he'd have died at the swimming pool, most likely. Or if not he's dead somewhere else and not far off."

"I see," said Superintendent Graham. He paused, looking carefully again at each film in turn. "There's just one thing, Doctor," he said. "Do you notice that in the early films of the series there is a number at the corner and beside it a date and below that a name?"

"Yes. They are stuck on the outside of the plate before it is exposed."

"I see. Then why, on the last two, is the name omitted?"

Dr Faulkner took back the films and saw that this was so.

"No idea," he said. "Carelessness, I suppose."

"I wonder," said the superintendent, carefully matching two of the films against one another for size. It was apparent to all who watched that the nameless films were about half an inch shorter than the others. "Would it be possible to find out," Graham went on. "The numbers on these films are plain. There will be a record?"

"Naturally."

Dr Faulkner stared. It was not difficult to guess what the copper was after. Which might prove to be exciting.

He led the way to the X-ray department. Two Fernandan radiographers looked up the records. They failed to discover the two numbered films, though one of them remembered Colonel Wilberforce quite clearly.

"It's odd," said Dr Faulkner. A blank wall was the last thing he had expected. "Dr Grigg would know, I expect."

"Then I must trouble Dr Grigg to give me another interview," the superintendent answered.

"Or Stone!" the doctor exclaimed. "Dr Stone, the radiologist, I mean. He'd know, of course."

"But Dr Stone is on leave," one of the radiographers said. "In the Argentine, I think. He has relatives there."

Of course, the superintendent thought bitterly. They should have held Stone. He had been too plausible, with his account of the Nazi side of his family with which he had never had any sympathy. Or so he had said, in a low whining voice, sitting opposite the superintendent at police headquarters. True? Well, that seemed possible at the time. The radiologist was suffering from shock, certainly. He was frightened, too. This morning Graham thought he feared the murderer of his cousin. But now—

Why had they let the man go straight back to the hospital, agreeing not to spread the knowledge of his connection with the corpse further than it had gone already? Not to damn him with his colleagues. So he had slipped off, his arrangements for his leave having all been made weeks ago. His American citizenship was not in question, his American passport was in order. There was nothing they could have done to stop him except subpoena him as a witness at the forthcoming inquest. That would not have been easy, either. Anyone in the X-ray department could present the film of the broken neck. Identification? Well, yes. Dr Stone's leave would last a month. He would be back. Or would he?

Superintendent Graham sighed heavily. He said, "There is an assistant radiologist?"

"Oh, yes," one of the girls said. "I bring her to you?"

"Please."

It was a young woman who came in answer to this call. A San Fernandan, coffee-coloured, with spectacles, knowledgeable, efficient. She listened to the story, she looked at the films, she went to the tall cabinet of records. Presently she came back to the waiting men and said, "The early films relate to Colonel Wilberforce. The last two, without names, should not be in his file. There has been some mistake. They belong to a patient who died a week ago. I was asked before to trace these films, but could not find them. I remember the case. Both cases."

"Was Dr Stone asked to find them?"

"*I* was asked to find them. That is all I know."

"Was Dr Grigg involved in this search?"

"Dr Grigg?" She looked astonished. "Why should he be? It was not one of his patients."

"Colonel Wilberforce was his patient."

"But the man with this large aneurysm, the man who died, was not Dr Grigg's patient. Also he died at his own home. He had left the hospital. His own doctor told us of his death. I thought he might have taken his X-rays out of his file himself. They do sometimes. They think the X-rays belong to them, not to the hospital."

"Good God!" said Dr Faulkner, becoming more and more confused by these developments. "I remember that chap. Spectacular. In his own home, too. His wife jolly nearly died of shock, they said."

"Everyone knew of it, then?" said Graham. "Dr Stone? Dr Grigg?"

"Why yes. They must have."

"Then, as I said before, I must speak with Dr Grigg again and the sooner the better."

But this was not to be. Dr Grigg was called in all the wards, in all the departments, at the flat in the university residential quarter where he had been living. But he had already left to take all his luggage to the airport. He was expected back at the hospital to take leave of the senior staff and his other colleagues, but he did not appear. Superintendent Graham went to the airport, to discover that the doctor was booked for the night flight and due to leave in the late afternoon. It was not possible to hold him, either, but the superintendent decided to make sure that he did actually leave the island. Having done this he went back to police headquarters, a puzzled and resentful man.

But at least, he comforted himself, these two, radiologist and physician, poor performers in their trade or active conspirators, he did not know which, were out of the way. Instead he had young Dr Faulkner and efficient Miss Milward. With their help he seemed to have established, for what it was worth, that Colonel Wilberforce had not been so desperately ill as he was thought to be. What *was* it worth? he wondered.

CHAPTER EIGHT

In spite of her concern for her uncle Alison slept well that night. Her room was shabby but the essential fittings did work; the air conditioning kept her cool and when she turned it off in the early morning and opened the window the mosquito netting outside protected her from insect attack.

She got up early and wandered for a time in the neglected garden where only the flowering shrubs, bougainvillaeas, frangipani and hibiscus still flourished. Among the tall weeds there was a number of low bushes covered with yellow flowers that reminded her of a single rose or a hypericum. She visited the swimming pool, discovering at the far end, partly hidden by trees and bushes, a narrow path that led between them to a small gate, with beyond it a rough-surfaced lane. The gate was rusty, loose on its hinges, but unlocked. As far as she could see, without going outside it, the lane led in one direction to a low bungalow behind the hotel and to the busy main road in the other.

She turned back, giving this half hidden opening no special importance, but instead letting her thoughts and speculations remain with the swimming pool itself. It had been emptied, perhaps last night, perhaps earlier this morning, but it had not yet been cleaned, she noticed. Its floor of pale blue tiles was dotted with fallen leaves, some fresh, some old and slimy. And with the bodies of drowned insects large and small, a lizard or two, the swollen corpse of a rat in the netting that covered the drain opening at the deep end on the other side from the steps.

Looking down at all this, Alison shuddered when she imagined that other drowned relic floating among the leaves and the insects. But not drowned, really, Jim had insisted. Done to death and discarded, trapped at the pool, killed, as perhaps this other rat had been killed and discarded and would now be gathered up with the rubbish and disposed of finally.

A Nazi rat. She turned away towards the hotel, ashamed of the fierce resentment that burned in her; an old, conventional national rage, fixed by two wars; an instinctive anger against false, hysterical, arrogant attitudes. Particularly an old anger, hardly personal for she had been a mere baby at the time, but an old wrath like a smouldering bonfire, bursting into fresh flame because this now dead enemy had taken away the uncle she had come so far to see.

When she got back to the verandah outside her room she heard distant voices, not all Fernandan, and realised that breakfast was now being served and realised too that she was pleasantly hungry.

The dining room was already partly occupied. At a table near one of the windows three large men in loose summer suits were attacking piled bowls of cereal. At another table, set back against the wall, a neat dark woman in a sleeveless flowered cotton dress was sipping coffee.

As Alison went in the three men turned at once to greet her in deep American voices. She answered them cheerfully, murmured good morning to the dark woman, who bowed in reply and found herself a seat at a table for one near the other window.

Jim appeared very promptly, bringing an old red leather-bound menu that must have served the Gardenia Lodge Hotel for many years. Alison wondered if all the printed courses were really still offered. She consulted Jim on this point.

"You want them all?" he asked, with laughter in his voice.

"No, no, of course not." She was laughing too. "No. Just fruit juice, cornflakes, bacon and eggs, toast and marmalade, coffee."

Just what she'd been having on the ship and enjoying it. She looked up at Jim to see if he was surprised to find a woman eating a real breakfast, but he was not in the least surprised.

"Two eggs, Missy Wilb?" he asked.

"Oh no, one egg. And one rasher of bacon."

He screwed up his face at this, then relaxed.

"One egg, one strip bacon. They small strips, Missy Wilb."

"One will do nicely."

The breakfast was the best she had had since leaving South-ampton, the coffee delicious. No wonder Uncle Ben had stayed on in this queer, run-down place.

The Americans spoke to her again as they filed out of the dining room. Simple inquiries about her room, was it O.K. and her sleep, did she have a good night, did she find it too hot, too noisy? She smiled and nodded and shook her head. The con-versation was too trivial for spoken answers. Besides, they all talked at once and she could not have got a word in edgeways.

The other hotel guest, who had sipped two cups of coffee and crumbled a piece of toast, gave her a vague smile as she left the room, but did not speak.

Alison then noticed that the Mancinis had slipped in while she herself was eating and were now sitting at a table near the door to the kitchen, their heads close together, speaking rapidly in a language she did not recognise. They lifted their heads as she passed and Mrs Mancini said in her fluent, foreign-sounding English, "Good morning, Miss Maclean. I hope you like your room?"

"Yes, thank you," Alison answered and was passing when Mrs Mancini added, "You will tell us your plans later, I hope."

"My plans?" Alison was astounded. She had booked her room for two weeks. She had no other settled plans. Her immediate intention was to see Uncle Ben's lawyer, Mr Gopal. Afterwards, according to what advice he gave her, she meant to find the British consul, perhaps even the High Commis-sioner.

"I want to see Princeton first," she said, smiling. "I haven't thought of what else I should see. And of course it depends on my uncle."

"Yes?" Mr Mancini said on a rising note. "You know where to find him? He has been in touch with you?"

"Of course he hasn't," she answered. "But I hope to see him soon."

She walked away, leaving the Mancinis staring at one another in confusion and some alarm.

Alison went to the office and bought a morning newspaper from Paula, also two coloured postcards to send to her mother and a friend. She then asked Paula to make a call for her to Mr Gopal's office and walked away, saying she would take it in her room.

But when the call came through it was Paula's voice, explaining that there was no answer from the lawyer's office. Alison, chilled but not yet apprehensive, thanked her and rang off.

She decided to go to Mr Gopal in person. The address was in the telephone directory and of course there was Jim, who had taken Uncle Ben's letter to Mr Gopal and so could direct her to his office.

The waiter was discouraging. He said the office was a long way from Gardenia Lodge; she would need a taxi; taxis were very expensive.

"But there are buses," Alison protested. "I've seen them stopping just outside here."

"You would go in a bus?"

"I don't see why not. I go in buses at home."

She spoke boldly but with inner misgiving, for everyone on the ship had warned her never to go out alone in the evening and never to travel on the buses.

Jim smiled at her.

"Bus all right," he nodded. "Not in rush hour. That's now. I tell you when."

With a less than clear picture in her mind of where she was going, but with Mr Gopal's address written on a scrap of paper Alison set out half an hour later, after giving the morning rush hour plenty of time to finish. She found the bus stop not far from Gardenia Lodge with only three people waiting.

It was difficult to understand, she thought, why she had been given such dire warnings by her shipmates. The bus was

about half full when she got on, though it had filled up by
the time they reached the centre of the city. Her fellow travel-
lers were all Fernandans on this occasion, all cheerful, all
polite, the women dressed in crisp cottons, the men in dazzl-
ingly white shirts. No possible danger here, she decided, des-
pising her misinformers. Until she saw, at a junction of routes,
where the bus made a longer stop than usual, the brown slim
fingers of a hand flicking across the open windowsill beside
the seat in front of hers. She could not see the owner of the
hand, she decided, unless she got up to look out of the window
near her own seat. So she moved her handbag, that lay just
below the window, held it tightly on her lap and waited. The
flickering fingers moved to her window, searching antennae-
like, dipping down, sliding sideways, pausing, then moving on
once more.

Alison had been poised to grasp that hand if it came near her,
but she felt there was as little chance of success as in snatching
at a bothersome fly. The owner of the hand would have pulled
free and be into the crowd and away long before she could
get her head out of the window. So she leaned back in her seat,
somewhat disillusioned, but not really discouraged.

Jim's directions were clear, but her mission in person was no
more successful than the telephone call. The office, a modest
converted Victorian house in a terrace of similar houses, stood
in a side turning off the main street of Princeton. It bore an
unostentatious brass plate fastened to the door, giving Mr
Gopal's qualifications and hours of business. But there seemed
to be no one at home.

Alison looked at her watch. She had set it correctly as soon as
she was through customs after leaving the ship. The time was
well within those stated hours. If Mr Gopal himself was out,
surely a secretary or even an office boy ought to open the door
to inquire her business.

She knocked again twice, then paused defeated. A rich deep
voice behind her said, calmly, "Can I help you in some way,
Mistress?"

Alison turned. A stout figure, dressed in khaki uniform, with red tabs and a khaki cap bearing the words 'Tourist Guide' in red, was standing looking at her with a faint smile on his wide mouth.

"Yes please," Alison said, her confidence returning. "I am trying to find Mr Gopal, whose office this is." She pointed to the brass plate.

"Perhaps he only sees by appointment," the guide said, hopefully.

"There is no one answering his phone. I tried," she answered. The guide looked perplexed.

"I think you will have to write a letter," he said, slowly. "I think maybe Mr Gopal visits a client out of town."

"You'd think he'd leave someone in charge here," Alison said indignantly.

The guide shook his head. He had no further suggestion to make. But Alison did not expect one. She was already making up her mind to follow her second plan.

"Well, I see I can't get hold of him at present," she said, accepting this fact and laying no blame on the guide, he was glad to observe. "Perhaps you can tell me where to find the British consul?"

This was easy, a request often made by tourists in trouble over transportation, overspending, illness or some other difficulty. The guide's face broke into a relaxed smile. He said, "I show you. Follow me."

The consul himself welcomed Alison into his office. He had read the newspapers. He had made a few discreet inquiries in likely quarters. He was able to tell the girl that her uncle's whereabouts were still unknown.

"What we do know," he said, "and I believe the newspapers have now got hold of it, so I am entitled to pass it on, is that the man who was slugged and popped into the swimming pool was a Nazi, son of a Nazi, who tried to pass himself off as Colonel Wilberforce's nephew and failed."

"I've been told all that already at the hotel," Alison said.

"There were two of them. The other may be George, my cousin. He wrote to my mother. My uncle George, this one's father, is dead. My cousin George wanted money but of course Mummy couldn't give him any."

"Would you know your cousin if you saw him?" the consul asked.

"Inspector Vincent asked me that. No, I wouldn't. He's been in the States since he was ten. I was about two at the time. If I ever did meet him I wouldn't remember."

"No. How long is it since you saw your uncle, Colonel Wilberforce?"

"About five years. He came back for nine months. It was just after he'd bought his coffee plantation here, he told us. But he wasn't living in San Fernando. It was all rather mysterious."

The consul nodded. He knew of the old man's occasional visits to the island over the years he had worked in South America but he saw no point in describing them now.

"He's been living here just over a year," he said. "He hasn't been well. He's been attending the hopsital."

"I know," Alison answered. Uncle Ben had said as much in his last letter to her mother.

The conversation seemed to be fading. The consul, a greying, benign figure, continued to turn a fatherly eye on her but offered no further information. In desperation Alison said, "At least you can tell me where this coffee plantation is. That seems to be what each of the two men wanted to know when they saw Uncle Ben."

"I haven't the slightest idea," answered the consul. "At least I have a vague idea it is in the mountains to the north. Nothing beyond that. Surely your uncle's solicitor can inform you."

"But I told you! I can't get hold of him!" Alison cried. "His office is shut up and no one answers the phone."

The consul was sympathetic but had no solution for her problem except patience and persistence. Alison, remembering that Peter Grant was on his way from England, decided to put the whole matter in his hands when he arrived and rose to go.

"I think," the consul said, seeing her out, "your best course really would be to fly home. You don't want to be mixed up— Colonel Wilberforce has a way of surprising—"

"But he may be dead!" Alison interrupted. "Or in danger— The thugs who killed that man—"

The consul did not tell her that a feeling was going round in official circles that Wilberforce himself had got rid of the nuisance and was now in deliberate hiding or even was already out of the country. He simply smiled, said he was at her service any time and saw her off the premises.

Alison made her way to the principal shopping street, again helped by a tourist guide. She could do nothing now until Peter arrived so she decided to behave as a normal visitor and began to look about her with a real interest in her surroundings.

Princeton was a busy modern city, she found, with shops very like those in the West End of London, several big self-service stores, narrow-fronted dress shops, well displayed chemists' windows, shoe shops, travel agencies, banks. At the entrances of narrow side streets men with barrows sold mangoes, paw-paws and other fruits. The pavements were crowded with people of all ages, strolling, talking, looking at shop windows. It was all familiar, Alison decided, except the variety of colour in the faces about her; black preponderant, white infrequent, every shade of brown between.

Already she accepted it; she was in a foreign country, in spite of the prevailing British architecture, a mixture, as in England, of the styles of the last three hundred years. A foreign country, a foreign land, with a delicious hot sun like that in Greece shining from a sky of big white clouds floating on deep blue depths. Not the fierce white sky of Greece at midday, but a kinder, softer sky, just as the dark faces round her were, for the most part, kinder, more friendly than the sharp, clever, dark-eyed faces of Greeks.

Alison wandered down to the harbour side. The on-shore breeze was warm, little waves lapped against a short pier where people strolled to and fro. She joined them, looking along the row of berthed ships to where the *Benito* had sailed in the day before. But the vessel had already left, bound for Freeman's Bay on the other side, the Atlantic shore, of San Fernando. She was to lie there for two days, taking on cargo, before beginning the return half of the cruise.

Alison felt a slight pang, a longing for the pleasant friends she had made on board, a half-amused memory of the young radio officer who had made tentative passes at her on those occasions when the ship's officers had helped to entertain the passengers.

She turned from the sea with her feelings of doubt, of anxiety, of loneliness, all renewed. As she began to walk back up the main street she no longer noticed the slow moving crowds, the laughing faces, the white façades of State buildings, set back behind smooth green lawns and beds of brilliant scarlet and yellow cannas. She saw instead, and winced to see, the seated groups of maimed beggars displaying their horrid deformities as they reached out for alms.

She had kept her eyes above pavement level before. Now she found it hard to raise them. The conditions she saw must have begun to develop years ago, under British rule. Had nothing been done for these wrecked bodies, many still quite young, almost children? Had they been hidden away before independence, deliberately avoiding medical aid, only emerging in the different climate of freedom? Or had they been ignored, criminally neglected? Were they better off, sitting against the plate glass windows of modern shops, making a living from the passing crowds, then they would have been, mended to some sort of mobility, capable of some low-paid job in some dingy place or alone in a broken-down shack? She shuddered as she passed slowly along, dropping sixpence here and there into a skinny hand to salve her conscience.

At the end of the street there was an open square with public gardens at the centre, filled with flowers. Here gardeners were setting sprinklers to work about the lawns and stout housewives sat on benches, their laden baskets at their feet, fanning themselves.

Alison joined them, resting and cooling herself and enjoying again the bright colours and general complacency. After a time, feeling restored, she began to make her way to the rows of buses drawn up at one side of the square. She was about to cross the road when a voice hailed her. The three Americans from her hotel were there, sitting in a large car at the kerb, smiling and waving.

She went across to them at once.

"Can we give you a lift any place?" the one who was driving asked.

"It depends where you're going," she answered smiling. "I was going to find a bus back to the hotel."

They all exclaimed in horror.

"You can't do that! Jump in. We're on our way there now."

The man next to the driver got out to make way for her, holding the door open politely until she was in, when he joined the third man in the back.

As they drove off Alison said, "This is very good of you. I'd forgotten the number of the bus I ought to take. I'm Alison Maclean."

A babble of names rose from the three men, which Alison sorted out, amidst a good deal of laughing, as Ray Leadbetter, Sam Forstal and Chester Bilton. Ray was driving.

"I suppose you've hired the car here?" the girl said, breaking the silence that had fallen after the exchange of names.

"Yah, we did that," Sam answered from the back seat. "But what makes you think so?"

"Well, it's a British make, isn't it?" she answered. "It has a right hand drive and they drive on the left here, as at home, so I was thinking how much easier for you than with an American car, so—"

"You are very observant, Miss Maclean," Ray told her, glancing sideways, not so much at her as at his companions behind.

"Alison," she said, not bothering to remark upon the compliment.

Conversation continued, desultory, friendly. The drive took so much less time than the bus would have done that the party reached the hotel again a good half-hour before lunch was due. Chester Bilton, younger, taller and the best looking of the three, suggested a swim before the meal. Ray agreed, Sam said he must write a few letters. Alison, feeling suddenly that the nightmare of her arrival was vanishing into appropriate unreality, agreed to meet the two men at the swimming pool in five minutes' time.

The cool, clear water now filling the pool, together with the cheerful companionship of the Americans, restored Alison's spirits. She swam well and knew it. Her neat dives and swift, elegant crawl won the applause she expected and though as a rule flattery never turned her head, on this occasion she was overwhelmed by such a complete return of her world to its normal course. The sinister, horrifying story that had met her when she arrived the day before seemed now quite clearly to be a matter for the police. Even her uncle's disappearance would, she decided, be found to have nothing to do with the murder, as it was described in the newspapers. An unfortunate coincidence which Uncle Ben would himself clear up, if he had not already done so.

Her mood of relief, of elation, lasted through lunch, through a brief siesta in her room, lying on her bed finishing a paperback novel she had bought in Trinidad during the ship's brief stop there and into an equally brief spell of letter writing, first to her mother and then to a cousin.

A knock on her door interrupted the latter, half-hearted effort. Ray Leadbetter stood outside.

"Miss Maclean—Alison," he said, smiling. "We're planning to join one of these short tours into the mountains tomorrow morning. We'd be delighted and honoured if you'd join us."

Alison went out to him on the verandah, shutting her door behind her, but forgetting to lock it.

"Why yes," she said, pleasantly excited. "Where do we go? How—?"

Ray was guiding her unobtrusively towards the office as she spoke. There he picked out a small pamphlet from a rack on the counter.

"Here we are," he said. "Conducted tour, nine a.m. to noon, Botanical Gardens, racecourse, old Governor's House, Moon Mountains, Barrack Hill—"

"Sounds lovely," Alison said. "Of course I'll join. On my own, of course, but in your company, I mean. I mean—"

"In our company, but quite on your own. I entirely understand," Ray laughed. Paula, watching with a grave face, totally without expression, took up a pencil.

"That's four, Paula," Ray went on. "Miss Maclean and we three."

"Yes, Mr Leadbetter," Paula answered, turning to plug into exchange. "If you wait one minute, I confirm."

A car drove up to the door of the office. Looking round idly, Alison recognised the man at the wheel. In a second she was outside the door, crying gaily, excitedly, "Peter! You couldn't have come at a better moment! You must join us! Tomorrow morning. Moon Mountains tour. You must meet—"

She looked round at the office just behind her, then at the verandah and the guest rooms, then back at Peter.

There was no smile on his face, no welcome for her. Surely he wasn't *still* angry? It hadn't even been a real quarrel.

He said, abruptly, "Where can we talk?"

"My room," she said, beginning to walk towards it. "On the verandah over here."

He followed, noticing that she walked straight in, had not locked it when she left. How long before? he wondered, but he did not remark upon it.

"I'm afraid I shall shock you," he said. "I did not expect to find you so—merry."

He spoke with contempt, paused, then went on, "I was told you were upset."

"I was," she answered, flushing. "Upset and absolutely mystified. Uncle Ben might have left me a note or even a message before rushing off wherever it is he's gone. Where is he?"

"If I knew I wouldn't be here alone," Peter answered, still resenting the glimpse he had had of her in the office, laughing up into the face of the dark-haired chap, who had vanished round the corner as she ran out towards the car. "I should be here with half the police of San Fernando with me, plain clothes johnnies and uniformed blokes—the lot."

"Why?" she asked, suddenly frozen, suddenly horrified with herself, suddenly back with the nightmare of yesterday and this morning.

She caught at Peter's hand, feeling her knees go weak with fear.

"Why?" she whispered again.

His old jealousy, restored by a new one, still rankled. He did not spare her.

"Because," he said slowly, "your Uncle Ben is suspected by every dick in this island of murdering Manfred Stein and possibly his own nephew, George Wilberforce, into the bargain."

CHAPTER NINE

"Oh, no!"

Alison's already established fear turned to swift anger. It was preposterous, unbelievable. The consul must have known and had not told her of these suspicions. Nor had Inspector Vincent. But they had evidently taken Peter into their confidence.

"How d'you know?" she cried, her voice shaking. The tears she had suppressed for so long were very near the surface.

"The police," Peter answered. "They've discovered from various witnesses who were in the grounds here the afternoon Manfred Stein came back—"

"He came back! After Uncle Ben had seen the real George?"

"Yes. They went up to the swimming pool to talk. Your uncle left the hotel later in a taxi. No one saw Stein leave."

Alison remembered the little gate behind the cubicles at the pool.

"They needn't have," she said. "There's a way out to the road behind the pool."

"Show me," Peter said, evenly. If this was correct the police must have seen it too, but they had not mentioned it that morning when he had gone straight to their headquarters from the airport. If they were going to be less than frank, he would have to go his own way, make his own inquiries.

This time Alison locked her room before leaving the verandah. Outside the office Paula was standing with two dark friends. She spoke as the two English visitors passed her.

"The Moon Mountains tour is fixed," she said. "They will call here for you."

"Oh good," Alison said and turning to Peter, went on: "Why not come, too? I'm sure there would be room. Wouldn't there?" she asked Paula.

"Your friend not staying here," the girl answered, coldly.

"Where are you staying, Peter?" Alison asked.

"At Four Paths Hotel. About a mile further out on this road."

"Four Paths have timetable for Moon Mountains tour," Paula said. "Must make reservations at Four Paths."

She turned away with her two friends and walking across the drive took them into the corridor that led to the dining room and the lounge.

Peter and Alison stared after her and then at one another.

"So now we know," said Peter. They both laughed happily.

"You'd better go and secure your seat for the tour, hadn't you?" Alison said.

"Want to get rid of me? Got a date with your Yankee boy-friend?"

"Don't be silly. They only got here yesterday, I think. I don't know them at all."

Peter was already moving towards his car. She stopped pro-testing, wondering why she had been moved to say so much. Did Peter really think she wanted to get rid of him? If he only knew how glad she was to see him.

She stood by the half-open window of the car, her hands resting on the edge of the glass.

"Why not go back to Four Paths and book for the tour and then come back here for dinner?" she said. "I'm sure there'd be no difficulty. The waiter, Jim, is a friend of mine already."

Peter leaned over to kiss the brown fingers clinging to the door of the car. As they did not move he put a hand over them to take them away, saying gently, "Not tonight. There are things—"

He looked up to see tears gathering in the violet eyes. Dis-appointment, hurt feelings, or just the continued aftermath of shock? It would be easy to comfort her—far too easy, he told himself savagely.

Aloud he said, "See you on the tour tomorrow morning. And Alison—don't *worry.*"

He drove off before she could answer or weaken his resolu-tion further. But he did not go far. Turning towards the town and pulling into the next convenient road on the left he parked the car, locked it and walked forward. He could see some of the Gardenia Lodge buildings between trees and shrubs at the margin of the road, so he was not at all surprised to find presently a narrow rough lane, unpaved, that led in the direc-tion of the hotel. It took him, as he expected, to the small gate behind the cubicles at the swimming pool. What he did not expect to see was a tall middle-aged black Fernandan, search-ing the ground just inside the gate.

As Peter already had his hand on the rusty latch when he caught sight of this figure and as the latter came sharply upright while his right hand went to his trouser pocket, the young man decided to explain himself at once.

"I am in Princeton to look after Miss Maclean," he said, quickly. "Peter Grant's the name. I think you work at the Gardenia Lodge."

There was no positive response to this, no movement at all of limbs or features. A trifle chilled, Peter wondered if he had made a major blunder.

"You are Jim—Jim—" Alison had not given him the waiter's surname, nor had he asked for it. He began to feel very foolish, but no longer at all alarmed, for the man had taken his hand away from his pocket and it held only a crumpled packet of cigarettes, one of which he took out and stuck unlighted in his mouth.

"Hulbert," said Jim, with dignity, but in a tone muffled by the cigarette. Peter took out his lighter and snapped it on.

"Hulbert," Jim repeated, lighting his cigarette, and now offering the packet to Peter, who refused.

"Mr Hulbert," Peter said, "I am here to look after Miss Maclean, as I said, but to do that I must find her uncle. Can you help me?"

"You tell me who you are. Then maybe I help."

It took some time, but Peter during his long training in the law had cultivated patience in dealing with clients, so often confused, distressed and ignorant. Though Jim was none of these things, his use of English was Fernandan and therefore not altogether easy to follow, while his general outlook and ways of thought were altogether strange.

In spite of this the interview went well, Peter decided. It was lucky he had come across the waiter where and when he did, quite by chance. Or was it by chance? He asked Jim, who answered vaguely, "Two men come this way. They not go back. Mas'r Wilb go out this way. He not come in."

"With the two?" Peter asked eagerly.

"No, man. After they two."

"How d'you know?"

"Little small rain, after they two, fore Mas'r Wilb."

"Do you understand all that?"

Jim shook his head sadly and Peter turned away. He went back to his car and began to turn it in the road. He was about to drive off again when he saw Jim standing at the mouth of the lane with a hand upraised. Peter moved back to him, leaning from the car to hear what he was saying.

"Mas'r Grant, you not see Mas'r Gopal? That Indian he know most all Mas'r Wilb business."

"Mr Gopal seems to have disappeared as well," Peter told him.

Jim shook his head but said nothing. He was still shaking his head and scratching his greying woolly hair when Peter glanced at him in the back mirror before he turned into the main road.

A minibus called at Gardenia Lodge Hotel the next morning at nine o'clock. Alison was already looking out for it at the office but the three Americans were late. They arrived running, to the surprise of the stout black driver who had lighted a cheroot and was prepared to wait until they chose to appear.

They piled into the front seats of the bus disputing who was to sit next to Alison and finally asking who she would have.

"None of you three," she said gaily. "I'm reserving this seat for an English friend of mine who turned up yesterday. He's staying at Four Paths Hotel. He said he would book on this trip. I suppose he has?" she added, turning to the driver. "A Mr Peter Grant. Four Paths Hotel."

The driver pushed his chauffeur's cap to the back of his head, took a list from his pocket and consulted it.

"Grant?" he asked, using a flat 'a'. "Yeh, yeh, I got him down here. We go now to Four Paths then on to Crossways."

"Full house?" asked Ray, who had by now seated himself directly behind Alison.

"That so, man," said the driver, throwing his unfinished cheroot into the drive and starting his engine.

Peter was standing at the door of Four Paths Hotel when the minibus drew up there. Alison felt a pang of envy when she saw the well-kept garden and generally prosperous appearance of the place, but she remembered that the sole reason for her engaging a room at Gardenia Lodge Hotel was because Uncle Ben was living there. It was equally natural that Peter, in San Fernando to make inquiries, would prefer to have his base a little further away.

He got in beside her and she introduced him at once to her new friends. At the next stop the remaining seats were filled by a party of medical Americans, a doctor and his wife, who was a qualified nurse, and a woman friend of theirs, a masseuse. They explained these avocations as they introduced themselves.

The driver said, "We go first by the race course, then past Governor's House, then to Botanical Gardens, where we stop twenty minutes. You get out, see flowers. Please to tip guide, two dollars American, five shillings Fernandan."

The tourists exchanged glances, some amused, others rueful. But they said nothing and the drive began.

Alison, whose seat was beside a window, was far too interested in looking at the passing scene to talk to Peter until, the race course behind them, they stopped outside Government House for those with cameras to take their photographs of it. It was a white dignified building, surrounded by banks of flowering shrubs and smooth lawns and beds of bright flowers. Alison got out to take the expected picture, then rejoined Peter who had stayed in his place. As the driver had also left to stretch his legs and talk to a gardener just inside the low boundary hedge, they had the little bus to themselves.

"Was it easy to get your place on this trip?" Alison asked.

"No problem. But I still can't raise Gopal. No answer from his office. He lives above it with an extension from the office phone, Inquiries told me."

"The police—"

"Have been in and found the place empty. All quite tidy. Just as he must have left it."

"Perhaps he and Uncle Ben are together somewhere."

"I very much doubt that."

"You aren't being very helpful, are you?"

They stared at one another, both suddenly angry, not so much with each other as with the strange, frightening circumstances that stood menacingly round and between them, spoiling a contact, unexpected and therefore delightful, that should have led to enjoyment, to pleasure, not to this tension, this bickering, this barely concealed rage.

Peter saw Alison's mouth tremble out of control. Inwardly he kicked himself for his boorishness but he had not thought of any other way of stopping her questions and conjectures. The three Americans had taken their pictures very quickly, he had noticed, and had returned to the minibus, taking up positions almost like a well-trained team, from where they could watch and perhaps hear everything that passed between him and the girl. At all costs he must keep to his role of English legal adviser, sent out as a representative of the firm that had looked after the Wilberforce family for generations. He must not allow any new feelings to weaken this resolution. He must not take advantage of her present isolated position—Hell, he told himself, she had been lovely to look at and to be with in England. So why should he expect her to have less effect on him out here. Only here—

He turned away from her without a word and Alison told herself that the quarrel, or near quarrel, for it had been no more than that, in London, had put paid to their growing friendship, had even turned him into a near enemy. Perhaps he had another girl at home by now and was annoyed and bored to be sent on this mission.

She stared out of the window again as the bus filled up and went on its way. At the Botanical Gardens she moved away from Peter at the door of the glasshouses to join Ray Leadbetter and the young Chester Bilton. She walked between the two men at the head of the procession, listened to their questions and the guide's answers, laughed at the obviously standard jokes and out of the corner of an eye watched Peter's efforts to get into conversation with the American masseuse who seemed to be far from eager to make his acquaintance.

But later, when the minibus began to climb into the foot-hills, where a good macadam road wound up and away from Princeton, she could not help exclaiming at the magnificent piled heights revealed at every turn in the road, the sweep of the distant sea, the horizon hanging in mid-air now and below the band of deep blue a thick and tangled growth of tree and bush with the roofs of hidden shacks dotted closely every-where.

There was one viewpoint where cars could pull off the road on to flattened earth. Here the driver made another scheduled tourist stop and gathered his passengers about him to explain not only the beauties of the distant scene, the view of the shipping in the great natural harbour, the factories on the water's edge beyond the town, but also the miles of shack-strewn hillside where people lived in hovels of their own making, while they waited for the flats or houses the govern-ment was putting up for them.

"Coming in off the farms in the mountains," Chester Bilton told Alison, standing at her right elbow, ignoring Peter who had come quietly up to her left side. "An old, old story. Can't keep them away from the city. Fast as they settle them there's more coming down."

"What happens to the farms?" Alison asked.

"They never grew enough. Subsistence line."

"Except for the plantations," Peter suggested, breaking in deliberately.

"Bananas and sugar cane?" Chester smiled. "Not up in the mountains. They're down along the big rivers in that main valley where the railroad lies. I believe they have onion fields up in the hills and some cocoa and spices and—of course—coffee."

Alison looked quickly at Peter, but he was gazing seawards and did not seem to have heard.

"They say at the hotel your uncle has a coffee plantation," Chester went on.

"Yes," Alison said. "He has."

"That's very interesting. Over this way, is it? Are you going to point it out to us as we go?"

Peter interrupted, "The driver's beckoning," he said. "All aboard again."

He turned away and began to walk back towards the bus. Alison thought he spoke and acted as churlishly as before, but she said nothing and followed after a very brief hesitation.

Chester let her go, moving across to his friends as they joined the rear of the party.

"Well?" Ray asked before they were again within earshot.

"Nix. But *he* knows where it is, I think. She don't."

The minibus continued to climb; the clustering shacks were replaced by small terraced fields and little crops of maize or wheat or onions. Most of the houses beside these groups of fields were built of wood, perhaps on a brick or stone base. They had tiled or thatched roofs, not the corrugated iron covering the shacks. But the husbandry looked poor enough, the occasional lean donkey or cow brought cries of pity from the American women and grunts of disapproval from the men. The driver, who was always ready to explain or comment upon all they passed, pretended not to hear the latest criticisms.

When they swung off the main road and began to climb an even steeper earth-packed track he began to talk again.

"We go now visit Barrack Hill Hotel. From hotel garden we see old barracks for English soldiers, built seventeen hundred and four. Soldiers had to walk from harbour with all their stores and arms, all way up to the barracks."

"Why did they make them go so far?" the American doctor's wife asked.

"Princeton very bad at that time for diseases. Chief town was Santa Maria, old Spanish capital of San Fernando. You been to Santa Maria, mistress?"

He was answered by a mixture of 'No' and 'Yes' from behind him and evidently took this to mark the end of questions for the time being. So he concentrated on his driving, which was very necessary as the road continued to climb, unprotected at the outer edge and narrowing as they mounted the hill. Once or twice, however, he mentioned the country houses of important members of the present government, pointing out their luxurious gardens, with swimming pools and fruit trees and here and there a descending set of terraced fields covered with the low bushes of the coffee plant.

Alison said, "My uncle, Colonel Wilberforce, has a coffee plantation somewhere in the Moon Mountains. These are the Moon Mountains, aren't they?"

"Oh yes, mam," the driver answered.

"Perhaps you know where I can find Colonel Wilberforce's plantation?"

The driver was astonished.

"You ask me where you find this coffee. You not know that?"

"No, I don't," Alison answered. She was aware of Peter's heavy foot pressing on her unprotected toes and hoped he was not ruining her white sandals. She did not intend to obey the signal, however.

"Ah'm sorry, mam. Ah can't tell you."

All eyes in the bus were upon her. She gave a wholly artificial laugh and said, "Never mind. I'll ask him when I see him."

The driver spun his wheel, the bus climbed off the track up an even steeper gravelled drive and stopped outside a low white-washed wooden bungalow.

"Barrack Hill Hotel," the driver announced. "Fifteen minute stop. Rum punch in bar."

The punch was excellent; the two white hostesses very welcoming. But the hotel did not seem to have any resident guests at all. None but themselves sat under the shady umbrellas in the delightful garden, no one passed through the bar or the comfortable lounge beside it. Many bedroom doors stood open, but in none was there any sign of an occupant.

While the party sipped their rum Alison found herself surrounded by her American friends, while Peter, she noticed, had settled down between the doctor and his wife. Later she managed to escape from her companions with the excuse that she wanted to take her camera round the garden.

"That little old plantation your uncle cultivates?" Sam Forstal asked, making way for her to pass him.

Alison blushed, was furious with herself for so doing and felt her cheeks burn more fiercely still. She shook her head and tried to laugh.

"I haven't a clue," she managed to say as she left the group.

"She knows," Sam said in a low voice, watching her move away.

Ray screwed up his face.

"I still doubt it. He does, maybe."

"He's gone after her," Chester told them. "We better move, too. Check on that map while they're out of our way."

Alison explored the garden, taking photographs of the flowers, the lily pool and distant views of the surrounding hills, where poui trees made brilliant splashes of gold among the green of leaf thickets.

"Those are the old barracks on the opposite hill," Peter said behind her and went on at once. "Take the picture. Don't look round."

She did as he asked because his voice was the friendly, confiding sound she had grown to need, perhaps to love, in England, before the party that broke the growing bond between them. She heard footsteps behind them, was aware of several people passing. Then they were gone. All except Peter, who now put an arm across her back and let his hand rest on her shoulder.

"Your US friends are looking for Uncle Ben's plantation," he said. "I think perhaps that's why they are up here to-day."

"How on earth—?" She was puzzled, indignant, because the trip had not seemed yesterday to be based on any ulterior motive. But Peter's hand pressed a little more closely and she could not deny his authority.

"Go on," she said, meekly.

"We've got to play this thing very quiet, very cool," he said. "Your Uncle Ben understands trouble. He's had plenty. If he's still alive he's capable of dealing with it. But he's a sick man, Vincent tells me. Not desperate. That was another bit of dirty work—"

"Peter!" Alison broke in. "I don't understand one single word you're saying. Uncle Ben—"

"Hush!" he said, dropping his arm to his side. "We'd better move on. They're coming back. Don't trust anyone, that's all. Be friendly and all that. But don't talk about Uncle Ben—to anyone."

She had recovered when they moved away. She fastened the case of her camera and said, firmly and deliberately, "I shall talk to Jim. He likes me and he was—is—Uncle Ben's friend."

Peter did not answer and very soon the call came to get back into the minibus. As they drove away they all began to talk about the delights of Barrack Hill Hotel, flourishing the brochures they had been given by the two young women who had served the punch.

"I didn't get one of those," Alison protested.

"You didn't? We had them given out at the door as we left."

"I didn't go inside. The garden was too lovely."

There was general mirth.

"You English and your garden," the masseuse said, gaily. "Take mine. I'll never come this way again, that's for sure."

Alison took the brochure and dropped it in her bag. She talked to the American woman until the bus came to its next stop at an old colonial building, once a planter's dwelling, now turned into a non-residential restaurant and road house.

Another welcome, another beautiful garden, this time, since they had come down from the mountains into a narrow valley, enhanced by a shallow rocky stream running through the middle of it. There were banana plants here, tall bright green leaves and in their midst a strange curving stalk with a purple and red flower hanging from the end of it. There were flower beds filled with roses, petunias, gloxinias, schizanthus and the yellow-petalled flower the guide at the botanical gardens had called alamanda.

"This place is the Alamanda House Hotel," the masseuse said. "I guess they've always had this flower in the garden from old colonial times."

"I must tell Peter," Alison said, looking about for him.

But he was not in the garden and when she walked back into the hotel he was not there either.

"Looking for Mr Grant?" asked the doctor, who was making his way towards the garden. "He's gone, I think."

"*Gone?*" Alison was astonished.

"He paid our driver and went over to a car with several—er—Fernandans in it," said the doctor's wife, dwelling a little on her description. "I think he asked them for a lift. Anyway they opened their car door and moved up to let him in."

Alison made a great effort to nod casually.

"I know he had an appointment in Princeton," she said. "We are quite a bit over our time, aren't we?"

She went with them back into the garden, feeling lost, lonely, apprehensive. The three Americans hurried towards her. They had a fourth man with them now, a big fair-haired man with a wide mouth and small sharp grey eyes.

"Miss Maclean, may I present Gary Wilkins," Ray Leadbetter said. "Gary, this is a fellow guest at our hotel, Miss Maclean."

"Alison," she said bravely, looking up at the stranger with what she hoped was an appealing smile.

CHAPTER TEN

The minibus took the tourists back to their respective hotels at the end of the morning. The American medical party said goodbye to Alison in a guarded manner, reluctant to express sympathy with such an icily controlled young woman, but eager not to appear unmoved by her predicament. How strange, they decided among themselves afterwards, for a young man to dare to go off like that without a word to the lady he was squiring. How discourteous, how bold, how unfeeling, how totally un-American. And the girl, too. She was not indifferent but she was not afraid; she was just downright furious, with a cold, silent anger quite outside their experience. Unnerving, really.

As for Alison her commonsense told her that there was probably a very good reason for Peter's sudden defection. But he should have warned her, not let her down, humiliated her before these strangers. Her Scottish pride could not take it. While behind her rage her growing absorption in Peter, his voice, his presence, his gestures, his infrequent touch, clamoured for recognition, demanded the true, frank declaration that whatever he did, wherever he was, however little his regard for her, she loved him and the love was growing every hour.

She struggled with herself and her anger and with a set face and frozen eyes chattered about nothing with her three new, attentive friends, who were as mystified as she was over Peter's action, and just as baffled by it. But as they agreed among themselves when Alison had walked away to her room, the English were always unpredictable. It came of this crazy cult of eccentricity.

With a shower, a change of clothes, a lunch for which she found she had a good appetite and was egged on by a delighted

Jim, Alison's better nature came back to the surface. Also her curiosity. She made a date with the eager and flattering trio for a swim before tea and then went back to her room to ring up Peter at the Four Paths Hotel.

But now she was met by another shock. Mr Grant was not there. No, they could not take a message. Mr Grant had checked out at the end of the morning. No, they did not know where he had gone. He had made the decision in a hurry, had packed his bag immediately and left before lunch. Thanking the voice at the other end of the line, Alison put back the receiver, laid her head on the dressing table and began to cry.

Her rage had now quite gone, washed away by frustration and a growing fear, less for herself than for Peter. It was totally unlike him to behave impulsively, impossible he would deliberately let her down. So whatever it was that had made him leave her so suddenly at Alamanda House and that still prevented him from telling her why he had done so, must be a serious development. He might be in danger and unwilling to involve her in it. She tried to tell herself not to be melodramatic but it was no good.

When her tears had dried she persuaded herself that since patience was not one of her virtues she must think of some way to find Peter. The consul had been kind but also very wary. He would almost certainly suggest once again that she had better give up and fly home. If she again refused, as naturally she would, it might be in his power to make her go or rather to arrange that San Fernando would consider her persona non grata.

But the police, particularly Inspector Vincent, had been kind and considerate. There was no reason why she should not put her problems to him; both her present defencelessness and Peter's possible danger.

It was very hot indeed on the bus going into the town again but there were hardly any passengers on board. Alison enlisted the help of a tourist guide who escorted her all the way to the

door of the police headquarters. Perhaps he thought she had
a complaint to make and wanted to be sure she did not
broadcast it to the general public. Perhaps he thought she was
mad but was not prepared to take responsibility for her. It
was unlikely that he knew who she was or that he guessed
her purpose. He saw her inside the station, waited to hear her
ask for Inspector Vincent, nodded as if satisfied and left
her.

After a short wait Alison found herself greeted by Detective-
Superintendent Graham in his office. He offered her a chair
on the opposite side of his desk and let her explain without
interruption.

When she finished by asking for at least a third time where
Peter had gone he simply shook his head without speaking,
unlocked a drawer in his desk and took out an object that he
placed in front of her.

"Do you recognise your uncle?" he asked, quietly.

Alison gave a little cry of alarm and disgust. But she recovered immediately. She had read two newspaper accounts
of the finding of the body in the swimming pool and one of
the pathologist's report at the inquest. The mask had been
mentioned in all, but not stressed. Nor had it been photo-
graphed or produced in public.

She stared at it now, at the closed lips and nostrils, seeing a
nightmare likeness to her memory of a much loved uncle.
Superintendent Graham had to repeat his question several
times before she turned a dazed face to him.

"Do you recognise the mask, Miss Maclean? Miss Maclean,
do you recognise your uncle in this mask. Miss Maclean—"

"I'm sorry!" She turned to look at him. "I was remembering—it's different in a way, of course. This dreadful colour
and so thin and lined. But it is Uncle Ben. Oh I'm quite sure
of that. Quite sure."

Graham took up the mask and opened the drawer again to
put it back. But as he did so a knock on his door was followed
at once by the appearance of a young constable in uniform,

carrying a long envelope. Graham put the mask down on his desk, half-rising from his chair.

The young constable was astonished to see Alison sitting there; Graham was furious at being disturbed by an entry he had not expected. He exploded into abuse and reprimand. The lad stood shivering, trying vainly to excuse himself.

'Inspector Vincent, sir,' he began but was overwhelmed. Alison got to her feet.

"Is Inspector Vincent back?" she asked the constable, directly.

"Yes mam. Tell me bring—"

Graham, suddenly recognising the importance of what the boy held in his hand, became silent and strode round his desk to take Alison to the door. The constable stepped back, seized the door and came to attention, holding it open.

"I would like to see Inspector Vincent," the girl said, firmly. "You have not helped me over Peter—Mr Grant's whereabouts."

"I have neither seen him nor had any word from him." Graham told her. "But I assure you we are taking your story seriously. He seems to have left you in a hurry at Alamanda House. This suggests, doesn't it, that he saw something or someone he wished to avoid?"

"How could he?" Alison was impatient. "There wasn't anyone."

"No one you hadn't met before?"

"Well, only an elderly couple drinking iced water, it looked like. And a friend of the three Americans at my hotel."

"Who was that? I think you did tell me. Name of—"

"Gary—something. Wilson. Williams. No, I know. Wilkins." They had reached the outer door. A scorching wind blew in from the street, making Alison gasp. The prospect of finding her way back to the bus station and finding the right bus appalled her.

Graham saw her distress and relented, forgiving her for the

insult he felt she had offered him when she asked the constable about Vincent. She ought not to have spoken to that eager young lout with his urgent message from the inspector not yet delivered.

"I will send you back in one of my cars," he said, with a lordly gesture. "It is too hot for you to walk and the taxis like to rest at this time. There will be very few around. Wait here."

Looking back up the hallway as she obeyed this order Alison saw the uniformed figure of the constable moving in the superintendent's room and another figure beyond him, back towards her, vaguely familiar. Where was Inspector Vincent, she wondered. Perhaps with another witness or suspect. Why was she not allowed to speak to him? What was in the long envelope the constable had brought to Superintendent Graham? Probably some totally different case, she told herself. Why imagine Uncle Ben was the only missing person on this island? Only of course he wasn't. There was Peter.

She felt tears behind her eyes again, but a police car was drawing up at the door, so she walked down the steps with her head up, gave her address to the driver and climbed into the back, fanning herself with the handkerchief she had a moment before taken out for another purpose.

Graham went back to his room. The young constable was still there, waiting to deliver his message about Vincent, he supposed. The long envelope, that he now saw was stamped and franked, lay on his desk where he had left it when he decided he must get rid of Miss Maclean before he could get on with his day's work.

"Well?" he said, dropping heavily into his chair. "What is it?"

"Inspector Vincent, sir. Tell me bring you that letter came in parcel from Mr Gopal, Indian lawyer."

"In a parcel? But it's been through the post! Where is Inspector Vincent now?"

"He gone out. Maybe come back. I go see, sir?"

"Do that," said Graham, quietly. "Tell him if he is here that I want to see him immediately."

He did not have long to wait. Only just time enough to open the long envelope and discover inside it the new will of Benedict Bracegirdle Wilberforce, signed and witnessed and dated on the day the old man had left Gardenia Lodge Hotel, or rather the night before Manfred Stein's body had been found in the swimming pool.

"Well, Vincent," the superintendent said when the latter arrived. "What else did you get besides this?"

He held up the long envelope and added, before the inspector could answer, "Ready for posting but never got to a pillar box."

"No. Gopal's boy must have been waiting in his flat above the office. He came down with the parcel. There is a note from Gopal saying he has already sent the contents of his safe to his bank, but thinks you should have a copy of the will. The original is at the bank, too. The parcel was made up to look like a small bundle of washing."

"Had the boy been up there all the time?"

"He said he had orders not to answer the phone or open the door except to the police. From the window he had seen the lawyer in the street with a man he did not know."

"Who was that?"

"White man. Not young, not old. American clothes. The boy had never seen him in the office."

"Not old? Not Wilberforce, then?"

"Certainly not Wilberforce. He was sure the man was American, not British."

"How could he possibly know?"

"He opened the window to try to hear what they were saying. He said his master, that's Gopal, speaks English English and this man spoke American English."

"While the boy speaks Fernandan English, or mostly Hindi, eh?"

They both laughed. Graham described Miss Maclean's visit.

"Poor girl! She has mislaid her uncle and both her lawyers. I think she will very soon go home. I think we should encourage that. After all, she has now no friends in San Fernando."

"She has that Jim Hulbert at the Gardenia. He knows more than he will say. She has the three Americans at the Gardenia also. They are asking questions about coffee estates in the Moon Mountains. Particularly they want to find Colonel Wilberforce's coffee estate."

"Are they coffee planters?"

"They are not. Mr Ray Leadbetter is a promoter of business in the US. Mr Sam Forstal is a geologist. Mr Chester Bilton is a chemical engineer. I think they look for minerals in our mountains."

"You mean bauxite, don't you?"

"Maybe. They would not be the first."

"You think one of them came to Mr Gopal to get in touch with Colonel Wilberforce in order to buy his coffee estate? And Mr Gopal has gone with him to show him where it is?"

"Maybe. Or was it that other nephew of the old man? Jim says the second nephew spoke American. Also he wanted to have the coffee estate."

Graham thought this over before speaking in. Then he said, "We have four things to know. Where is Colonel Wilberforce and what is he doing? Where is Mr Gopal and what is he doing? Where is that American the girl calls Gary Wilkins, who knows the three Yankees and met her at the Alamanda? And where is the American-speaking George Wilberforce, who wants to get his hands on his uncle's coffee estate?"

"I think he is in the same skin as Gary Wilkins," said Vincent grinning. "I think the disappearing English lawyer, Peter Grant, recognised him and that is why he left the Alamanda suddenly this morning."

"I think so, too," said Graham. "It will be your next job to prove it, Vincent. Also to find out where he is, whether he took Gopal away or if that was the syndicate of three. We must know if their purpose is the same or different. That will be for me."

As an afterthought he added, "There is one more question. Why did Gopal not give me the signed will which he had in his safe when I first saw him about Stein's death?"

"Perhaps to make the copy he has sent you. The original is now at the bank."

"And what was in the message Jim took that night Wilberforce disappeared?"

The two men shook their heads over this but did not speak. Then Graham said, "Miss Maclean did not recognise this George Wilberforce, supposing he is Wilkins?"

"She has not seen him. Or only when she was a young child. Peter Grant saw him in London. He did not visit his aunt and her daughter. Only wrote to the aunt."

"That is a pity. She could have helped us. She thought she recognised her uncle from the mask. It upset her; she said he must look much older than she remembered him. And ill, very ill."

"You showed her the mask?"

Inspector Vincent was shocked. He thought this was a callous action. He had been rather disgusted by the mask. He remembered its effect on the women at Gardenia Lodge. But of course Miss Maclean was different from those women. Strange colouring, so tall and thin, from that cold, northern part of Britain called Scotland, that was covered in the winter by the frozen water called snow.

"I showed her the mask," answered Superintendent Graham, irritably. He resented the reproach in Vincent's voice, chiefly because he had really done it to test the girl's stamina.

He pulled open the drawer in his desk, to convince himself and the inspector that the thing was interesting—spectacular, perhaps—but held no real overtones of terror.

The mask was no longer there.

CHAPTER ELEVEN

In spite of the fact that the police car brought her to the Gardenia Lodge Hotel far more quickly than she would have been able to get there by public transport, Alison found the swimming pool deserted, the lounge verandah empty, no voices to be heard in the rooms near her own.

She went to the office to buy the day's newspaper, not having had time to do this before setting out for the Moon Mountains that morning. Paula was there, quiet and unsmiling as ever. There were no newspapers left unsold, she told Alison, but reaching behind her to the table where her assistant sat, she folded and handed over the counter a copy that Alison supposed was her own.

"Thank you so much," she said, not quite sure if she ought to offer to pay for it. "When shall I bring it back?"

Paula shook her head.

"I read it all," she said gravely. "You keep it, Miss Maclean."

"Thank you so much," Alison repeated and went on. "It's very quiet just now. Is everyone out?"

It was a silly way to ask for the three Americans, she realised, because she had already noticed that their car was not in the drive so of course they had gone out again.

'Mr Leadbetter out and take Mr Bilton. Mr Forstal take siesta, I think. Better to take siesta, Miss Maclean. Less tiring when the sun so high."

Aware of her heightened colour, because she had felt her face flush as she remembered about the car, Alison's cheeks burned even more fiercely now. She had a sharp impulse to smack the smooth cream-coloured face on the other side of the counter. Anything to bring a spark of pain or anger to the blank, expressionless eyes. But she beat down her rage, gave an artificial, rather high laugh and saying, "I think I'll have a swim instead. Many thanks for the paper," swung round and began to leave the office.

Paula's voice reached her again. "Your American friends have visitor tonight at dinner. Mr Gary Wilkins. And ladies from Barrack Hill. Hostesses."

Alison nodded without turning and walked on.

Paula waited until she no longer heard footsteps in the drive, then reaching to the telephone exchange beside her, began to put in plugs and switch keys.

In her own room Alison read a few headlines, searched for and found a paragraph or two of English news and then laid the paper aside while she stripped. She put on a bikini, struggled into a bath robe, snatched up a towel. Company or no company she meant to have her swim.

Dropping her towel on a metal chair near the cubicles at the deep end of the pool she dived into the water and crawled quickly across to the far side, swung round and crawled back. During this time she had turned up her face to breathe at intervals but otherwise held it down in the water. She did not look up until she reached the side under the diving board. She then saw Peter Grant sitting on the metal chair with her towel over his knees.

Her first impulse was to call out his name in joy, in immense relief, in latent indignation. But he was watching her. He saw her face change from astonishment to pleasure to annoyance. He held out the towel towards her and smiled.

Alison swam to the steps, climbed out and went to him. He got up to drape the towel round her shoulders. She put up her dripping arms round his neck so that the towel fell away again. She said, brokenly, "I thought they'd killed you, too," and began to cry.

This was a reaction Peter had not at all expected. Here was his adored and much desired Alison in his arms, but soaking him to the skin. He tried to lift her head from his shoulder but only managed to squeeze a fresh shower from the thick cap of auburn hair he had so often longed to stroke. When at last she did look up he found himself kissing wet eyelids, cold wet cheeks and a cold wet mouth where salt tears running down had mingled with the strange taste of the swimming bath.

This treatment, helped by the warm sun on her back and Peter's warm body pressed to her front, soon brought Alison to her usual self. She took away her arms, leaned back and said, in unaffected dismay, "Oh darling, I've soaked you!"

"Not to worry!"

With a last, unsatisfactory kiss on the top of her head Peter let her go, picked up her towel and handed it to her. She spread it on the tiles near the edge of the pool and lay down on it. Peter pulled the chair nearer, took off his shirt and spread it in the sun.

They began to giggle. The nightmare background again receded. Until Peter remembered Alison's genuine concern.

"You really did worry about me?" he asked tenderly.

"Of course I did."

"I thought it was all off. Never been properly on, really."

"Why?"

"You know why. That party when you wouldn't let me drive you home. Your mother was quite agreeable. I asked her."

Alison sat up with a jerk.

"You didn't!"

"Of course I did. Why not? I had no ulterior motive. Seduction wasn't on that night, anyway. I was annoyed to think you suspected me of something I was consciously postponing."

"Big of you. I thought you thought I was just another chick that liked sleeping around."

"God forbid! Also I'm not exactly that sort myself, as I've explained. I go for quality, not quantity."

Alison lay back again and shut her eyes. The quarrel was over. There was, once more, a future entirely filled by Peter. She would have been quite ready to catch the next plane home if he was to be on it too. She no longer wanted to find Uncle Ben, solve the mystery of his disappearance, nor the secret of his coffee plantation if it really had ever held one.

However, there was still one thing that troubled her. Why had Peter left her that morning at Alamanda House without a word of explanation?

"What happened to you this morning?" she asked. "I thought you'd been kidnapped."

"I recognised the new American."

"Gary Wilkins?"

"Is that what he calls himself? In London he saw my firm as George Wilberforce, junior."

Alison sat up with a jerk.

"My crook uncle's son? The one who came here after the Nazi imposter? He can't be!"

"Why not? I recognised him, I tell you. We know he's on the island. Apparently came in on his own passport because no George Wilberforce has been through immigration or customs."

"How d'you know all this? His *own* passport?"

"Superintendent Graham, the American Embassy, the British High Commissioner. Yes, his own. He has American nationality."

"You haven't wasted your time! All that this afternoon?"

"While you slept out your siesta."

"I did *not*. We could have met at the police station."

She told him of Gopal's continued disappearance, the arrival of a parcel for Graham, her sight of the mask of Uncle Ben. She complained of Graham's secrecy over Peter's visit to him until she learned that she had been there before him.

"I don't understand how they failed to see that thing was a mask as soon as they got the body out," he said, staring at the water. "I'd have thought the join would show." She shivered, turning troubled eyes to Peter. "If it's lifelike, a real likeness of Uncle Ben, I mean, he must have aged a lot and be very ill. It's a horrid colour—the mask, I mean. Greyish-blue. Foul!"

"The body was probably much the same colour when they took it from the water," Peter said steadily, watching her. "I gather they had towels ready to drop over it, face and all. Then Jim fetched a sheet."

"You've been talking to Jim," she said.

He nodded.

"What will you do now? Where are you staying?"

"At the Marshalls'. You've met him. British consul. Actually he's a cousin of my mother's. That's partly why I'm here and not one of the senior partners. But I booked in at Four Paths to be nearer this place."

It all sounded very reasonable. Again Alison felt the tension loosening until she remembered what Paula had told her. Her watch was in her room. She snatched at Peter's dangling wrist, saw the time and jumped to her feet.

"I've just remembered! He's coming to dinner here. Paula told me. What shall I do? Pretend I don't know who he is?"

"George coming here! Christ, he might be here now!"

Peter snatched up his shirt and struggled into it, shuddering as it clung damply to him.

"Can you get away without anyone seeing?" she asked anxiously.

"Yes, yes. That's not the point. Look, you'd better get dressed and come out with me at once. I've got the car in the lane behind here. I'll wait."

A car turned into the drive as he spoke. It was hidden by the mango trees but the cheerful voices of the men getting out of it reached them, recognisable, unmistakable.

"He's there now!" Alison said. "Oh God, did you hear that? They're all coming up to swim. I can't even get back now. They'll change in the cubicles. They always do."

"Meet me after dinner then," Peter said quickly. "At the little gate behind here. No, don't come now! Just watch."

He was gone, slipping between two bushes on the path Alison had noticed before. She turned to pick up her towel and put on her bath robe, delaying her actions, waiting to hear his car come to life, wherever he had hidden it. When it did so and she heard it move away she began to leave the pool.

Peter had been just in time, she decided thankfully. Four figures were already crossing the loggia. They waved their towels and bathing trunks when they saw her, so she stopped, waiting for them to arrive at the pool.

"Beaten us to it!" Ray shouted as they drew near.

"Beaten you by ages," she said, catching back the exact time, since she had no watch with her. "I've just had my swim. And dried off in the sun."

"Shucks," Chester said. "Come on in again."

"Race you to the other end!" called Sam, who had already shed his outer clothing and appeared on the diving board all ready in bathing shorts.

Gary Wilkins said nothing. He was staring at Peter's tie that had fallen from his trouser pocket where he had stuffed it clumsily. It lay now like a graceful curved snake halfway between the tiles beside the swimming pool and the almost hidden opening in the bushes.

Alison saw him staring, saw the tie and saw the dark look that swept over his face as he stared. A look so compounded of evil enraged that she flung herself away into the water with ungainly spread limbs and a great splash that raised a shout of laughter from the three Americans. As she set off after Sam she told herself one more chilling fact. Gary, or George as she now called him to herself, must know that hidden path as well as Peter did. He knew from the presence of the fallen tie that she had not been alone at the pool and he knew which way her companion had gone. It was not going to be easy after all to join Peter at the little gate after dinner that night.

It was not even necessary. There was plenty of time, she told herself bitterly, while she was shut up in her room dressing for the meal, for her cousin to make his own plans. But she was not prepared for his disarming approach to her on the lounge verandah as she sat there alone sipping a planter's punch to brace herself for further shocks.

He had not swum with the other three, but he must have

been with them after they left the pool, she decided. She thought of making an excuse to take her drink into the lounge but he stopped her.

"Please Miss Maclean—Alison," he said, one hand on her arm, an anxious look in his eyes. "I can call you Alison, can't I? I've a right to, really, because we are cousins. Honest. No, don't go away! I want to explain. I owe it to you to explain, don't I?"

She did not know how to answer this, so she sat still, waiting for the explanation that would be partly true but not the whole truth, she felt sure. Of course he had to acknowledge he was George Wilberforce. Hadn't he been to Gardenia Lodge before? Wouldn't Paula and Jim recognise him if none of the others did?

"I came to San Fernando to see Uncle Ben," George went on. "This was after I'd been to England to find him. Your mother wouldn't see me, sent me to your lawyers. They put me off too, but they let out Uncle Ben was living here."

Lie number one, Alison counted. He knew where Uncle Ben was all the time. Peter's firm would never have given him the address.

"You saw Uncle Ben, didn't you?" she asked, steadily. "In the afternoon of the day that young German came and Uncle Ben saw him."

A spark gleamed in George's muddy, grey-green eyes.

"Wasn't it the next day our revered uncle saw that guy off for good?" he asked.

"Certainly not. He came again but I'll never believe Uncle Ben killed him. He's old. He has a dreadfully bad heart. He *couldn't* have done it."

"He has a reputation," said George grimly. "Who told you all this?"

"Inspector Vincent," said Alison, not quite accurately. "I've seen the police several times since I got here."

George made no answer to this. He seemed to be considering.

"I came out partly for the voyage," Alison went on. "Partly to see just how ill Uncle Ben is. You came in from the States, didn't you? Also to see Uncle Ben. Why? And why do you call yourself Gary Wilkins?"

He was not at all put out.

"That's my business name," he answered readily. "Wilkins, partners. My mother's family name. The original Wilkins, her uncle, is retired now but the firm travels as Wilkins."

"Surely your passport isn't Gary Wilkins, is it?"

The sudden tightening of his mouth frightened her, so that she repeated her former question. "Why did you come to see Uncle Ben?"

He hesitated. Watching him Alison could not decide if this was genuine reluctance or a piece of calculated timing. When he spoke she knew it was the latter.

"Same reason as you," he said. "His health. To fix a few things with him before he died."

"Such as?"

"Such as what?"

"The few things. You really want to know if he's leaving you anything, don't you, George? This poor little coffee plantation, for instance."

"Why poor?"

"Because coffee's on the way out here now, isn't it?"

"I don't think myself that Uncle Ben depends on the coffee."

"Don't you? Then what does he depend on? Buried treasure?"

She spoke at random, meaning to stall, meaning to laugh him out of probing any longer for an account of what she knew of their uncle. But his reaction astonished her. His face grew white and tense, he leaned forward and again grasped her arm, but this time so strongly that she gave a cry and struggled to free herself.

"Hey, hey, what gives here?" cried a cheerful voice from the lounge.

George dropped his hand, turned away, seized Alison's glass and drained it.

"Family affection, Sam," she said, trying to laugh. "George has just told me he's my long-lost cousin from Ohio—Uncle Ben's nephew."

Sam did not seem at all surprised. He merely nodded and said in a quiet voice, "The girls are here, Gary. I suggest you invite Alison to sit with our party for dinner. The others have gone in already."

The girls turned out to be the two hostesses from the Barrack Hill Hotel. Alison recognised them and told them so. They smiled and said they recognised her, too. Jim moved the whole party to the central dining room table and they sat down three a side with Alison at one end. The solitary Fernandan lady came in late, made her usual bow of acknowledgment, ate a little and left early. The Mancinis came in, studied the scene for a few seconds and disappeared into the lounge, evidently intending to eat later when the noisy white party had left. In the meantime they would watch television. The dining room was momentarily flooded with background music and a loud voice, instantly cut down to a distant murmur.

Alison enjoyed the meal. She did not talk much, nor was there much opportunity for her to do so, since the others all spoke at once, no one apparently listening to anything that the others said.

The chatter ceased abruptly however when Jim came in carrying a sheet of paper which he placed beside Alison.

"Paula take message on phone, Missy Maclean," he said, in a low voice.

She read it, then turned to George, though she guessed he knew it already.

"This is from Peter Grant, my lawyer, who has come over about Uncle Ben's affairs. He wants me to go up to Barrack Hill at once. Uncle Ben is there, very ill indeed. They've got a doctor who says it's urgent."

She rose as she spoke, fixing her eyes on the older of the two hostesses.

"Did you know Colonel Wilberforce was at Barrack Hill?" she asked. "Was he there this morning? Why wasn't I told?"

The hostess had risen, too. She looked bewildered, inclined to be angry.

"Of course I didn't know! Nor that you were his niece. Olive and I only work there when tourists are coming up. It doesn't belong to us."

"It belongs to Colonel Wilberforce," said Olive. "Mrs Jackman runs the residential part. You've seen her name on the brochure, or didn't you get one? But the real owner is Colonel Wilberforce, your uncle, if you really are his niece."

"So now we know," said Ray Leadbetter, quietly.

The three friends turned their heads to look at George, who was on his feet too, working up a great act, Alison thought.

"I'll take you up there at once," he said to Alison. "Get a wrap. It'll be cold in the mountains."

"Have you got a car?" she asked, desperately trying to think how she could get in touch with Peter.

"Sure, sure. Hurry, honey. We may be too late."

For a second, as she went quickly from the room, Alison thought her best plan would be to go out to the gate by the swimming pool and hide there until Peter arrived. But she knew it was too early and when she thought of George finding her there, as he surely would, since it was the first place he would think of searching, she knew she dared not risk it. Besides, the message might just possibly be true. She would have to go. She would have to find some way to tell Peter where she had gone.

Once again Jim Hulbert came to her aid. He moved silently to her side as she was unlocking the door of her room.

"That message," he said in a low voice. "Paula got no message over phone. That message come from Mas'r George. No good message. You not go to Barrack Hill, Missy Wilb—"

She stopped him with a hand on his arm.

"Listen, Jim. I think I have to go. But Mr Grant was going to meet me here—"

She explained the arrangement made at the swimming pool.

"Will you tell Mr Grant what has happened, where I've gone and why?"

"Explain, yes. But much better you stay here and not go. Therese keep you safe. Up at Barrack Hill—"

He broke off, shaking his head, moving his hands in profound disapproval of her obstinacy. But Alison hurried away from him into her room and when she left it again a few minutes later he had gone.

There was only one light shining in the Barrack Hill Hotel as they approached it, but another went on over the porch as George drew up to the door. Before he had left the car the door opened and a tall man stepped forward.

Alison, who had stayed in her seat, waiting to see what George would do, shrank back at sight of the stranger. He was Fernandan, dressed in an old-fashioned black frock coat, with a high stiff white collar and a black tie. He said something in a low voice to George, then, putting him aside with a large dark hand, approached the car.

"Miss Alison Maclean?" he asked, but did not wait for an answer. "I am sorry to give you bad news. Your uncle had a severe seizure four hours ago. I was sent for. I could do nothing."

"Are you trying to tell me he's dead?"

Alison heard her voice trembling; she felt too weak to move. She saw George begin to walk back towards the car, heard his voice, heard his false sympathy.

"We're too late, Alison. Perhaps it was the best for him. Dr Silver tells me he didn't suffer. He was unconscious from the time he collapsed."

Alison wrenched open the door of the car and got out.

"Where is Mr Grant?" she asked the tall man. "The message came to me from him. My cousin was kind enough to drive—"

"Mr Grant?" The doctor seemed bewildered. With an impatient gesture she walked past him and straight in through the open door. The two men in the drive heard her call, "Peter! Peter, where are you?"

"Why the hell didn't you stop her?" George said, furiously. "Come on, before she makes more trouble. Damned, independent bitch!"

Alison had not left the hall. They found her there, white-faced now, all her fears justified, regretting she had not taken Jim's advice. But when the two joined her she forced herself to say, "Dr Silver, was it my cousin George here who called you in to my uncle? Not Peter Grant, who is my lawyer?"

At the word 'lawyer' the big Fernandan rolled his black eyes at George and frowned heavily, but he did not answer. Seeing she would get no help from either of the two Alison said, curtly, "Where is Mrs Jackman? I understand she is house-keeper here?"

Dr Silver said, "She met me at the door and let me in. Then she ran away. I have not seen her since."

Alison was furious. Did they think she was a complete moron?

"I don't believe a word of it!" she cried. "Not a word. I don't believe Uncle Ben was taken ill. I don't believe he's here, dead or alive. Why have you brought me here? What do you want, George? What idiotic game d'you think you're play-ing?"

Dr Silver moved back until he stood against the first door that opened from the hall. George looked at his cousin with cold eyes.

"I want this place," he said. "The hotel and the coffee fields. Uncle Ben wouldn't give them to me. But they belong to you now he's dead. You'll give them to me, Alison. You'll have to give them to me, won't you, my dear?"

The threat was stale cinema stuff, she told herself, the whole thing was bluff. Hang on until Peter comes. It couldn't be long before he did. Go on stalling, that was the thing.

"I must see his body," she said, trying to control her voice.

"I must be satisfied that he is really dead, first. It doesn't seem possible. All alone up here in the mountains. Those two girls—Ray and Sam and Chester—"

She saw George's face change as it had changed at the swimming pool. She dared not provoke him further. She turned to Dr Silver.

"Take me to him," she demanded. "It is only right that I should see him. You will be giving a death certificate, I imagine. I don't suppose you want me to question it at a coroner's court, do you?"

The two men exchanged a swift look, of inquiry, of command, of resignation. Then Dr Silver took her arm, opened the door behind him and led her in.

There was a shaded light on a table near a low bedstead. The light they had seen as they approached the house, she thought quickly. There was a sheeted form on the bed, the white cloth spread closely up to the neck, but leaving the head and face visible. Alison saw lined grey wrinkled skin, thin greyish-blue lips, parted a little to show a row of teeth gleaming between. Closed eyelids, sparse grey hair above a wrinkled forehead.

She swayed where she stood. It was the face of the mask she had seen on Superintendent Graham's table, but the mouth of the mask had no opening, this had. The mask Graham had shown her was taken from a locked drawer. So this was Uncle Ben himself, dead indeed.

Her forehead went cold, her eyes darkened. She heard herself cry, "You've murdered him!" and felt hands lowering her to the floor.

CHAPTER TWELVE

Jim kept the rendezvous punctually at the gate near the swimming pool. When Peter drew up in the road outside he went forward at once down the lane, a shadow moving against dark bushes. He had changed his waiter's white jacket and shirt for a black sweater and a black jacket. He went quickly round the car to the passenger side, opened the door and got in.

"I tell Mr Mancini I go see my friends, you know," he said with a wide grin. "True, Mas'r Grant, I think."

"Glad to have you with me," Peter said quietly, "but I was expecting Miss Maclean."

"She gone with Mas'r Wilb, young Mas'r Wilb. I tell you but we go quick, please."

On the way to Barrack Hill Peter listened to the story of the dinner party with the girls from the hotel and the message written out by Paula.

"But no telephone," Jim explained. "We hear in kitchen when Paula is talking. My wife, Therese, always hear. Tonight nothing but a message written on folded paper. So I read it," he said, simply.

"Good for you. I think we'd better hurry."

Bent on speed Peter concentrated on the road ahead. Though he had been that way twice already in the morning, in daylight, both going and coming, it was a different matter to drive along the same road at night, a moonless night too, with a dark sky and few lighted houses except far below in the valleys and behind where Princeton lay at the harbour's edge.

So intent was he on the final twists and turns that he scarcely noticed an oncoming car until it flashed upon him, seemingly from the hillside itself. He pulled out of its way just in time, felt his nearside back wheel spin on the verge, wrenched the wheel back again and stopped.

"Up here, Mas'r Grant," Jim's voice grated in his ear. "Sharp turn on right. Up to house."

Of course, the hidden drive, the steep hidden drive! Which Jim evidently knew well, too! Peter swore, put the car in bottom gear and ground his way to the front of the hotel. There was a dim light in one of the front rooms. As he stopped the engine a red glow broke out at the back of the house on the side nearest to this room.

"Holy Mary! Fire!" cried Jim.

They leaped from the car. The waiter sped on his long legs round the corner of the house. Peter rushed to the front door, found it unlocked and burst in.

The wide lounge hall was full of smoke. It was the place where his tourist party had drunk their rum that morning. The smoke thickened every instant, a fierce crackling terrified him. He called 'Alison' and there was no sound but the crackling, no movement but the smoke waves billowing round him.

Pulling himself together he remembered the light he had seen. A room beside the main door. He ran to it and flung it open. On the floor lay Alison, one arm flung wide, her dress bunched above her knees. On a bed a figure was stretched, covered entirely by a white sheet.

Calling loudly for Jim, Peter lifted Alison's limp form, thankful to find her warm and breathing, though deeply unconscious. He carried her outside and laid her on the grass beside the drive, turning her head a little to one side, propping it there with his rolled up jacket.

Jim came round the corner of the house panting and coughing.

"I put it out, man," he gasped. "Little small fire of wood with oil on. By stove in kitchen knocked over."

He caught sight of Alison and gave a cry.

"She's not hurt," Peter said. "At least I don't think so."

He could not enlarge upon these feeble words to Jim. But the whole situation, the house deserted except for a sheeted corpse, an unconscious girl and a fire starting by itself—

"I think some wicked man made that fire," Jim's voice cut into his frantic thoughts. "Maybe to burn Missy Maclean. We come too soon. He see car on road and run away."

"And nearly wrote us off as he did so," Peter said, rising to his feet. Alison's pulse was firm and regular and her breathing, too. She was in no danger. But George had brought her here and left her, obviously drugged, meaning her to burn. If he had harmed her in any other way—

He remembered the sheeted figure on the bed.

"There's a dead man in the room where I found her," he said. "Come on, Jim. We may as well see if there's anything there we can do."

When he uncovered the face of the corpse on the bed Peter exclaimed in astonishment and horror. He too had seen the mask in the Superintendent's office and he came to the same conclusion as Alison. Colonel Wilberforce had died as the urgent message for her had suggested.

But this time Jim was unmoved. He pulled the sheet down further, disclosing a brown chest and arms below the grey lined face and neck. In a few seconds the mask was off and now Jim cried out in anger and grief.

"That Mr Gopal! Mas'r Wilb's friend and lawyer!"

"This is murder!"

Peter ran outside again. Whoever had done this thing might still be near enough to attack again. It was clearly aimed at Alison. She must first have been convinced of her uncle's death and then left to burn together with a corpse that would be rendered unidentifiable by fire.

An evil scheme, but crazy. Live victims might die, but bodies did not burn so easily; not in a fire so badly organised in a bungalow of no more than twelve rooms that would burn itself out very quickly. A crazy amateurish act, but the cold-blooded wickedness behind it was not that of an amateur in crime.

The smoke had nearly blown away from the hall when Peter carried Alison back into the house and laid her down on two chairs that Jim had put together for her. She was stirring in his arms by this time and when Jim, always ready, always resourceful, handed him a cover from one of the hotel bedrooms and Peter began to spread it over the girl, she opened her eyes, recognised him and gave a little cry, remembering her terror.

Jim raided the hotel bar but Peter turned down alcohol for Alison since she was still clearly under the influence of some sedative drug. He sent Jim to find coffee while he explained to her what had happened. The latter came back very soon full of apology. The kitchen stove was unusable but there was some cold coffee in a jug of ice. If Missy Maclean could drink iced coffee—

Alison, her head swimming and her eyes still focussing badly, managed to sit up and sip the sweet cold brew that Jim had sugared with a lavish hand. She began to improve fairly quickly. Peter and Jim watched her, rewarding themselves with liberal tots of rum.

"What now?" Peter asked aloud. "We can't use the phone, the line's cut. We can go in my car, but we can't leave Gopal here." He turned to Jim. "Where's the nearest house we can use a phone?"

"Three mile down mountain. You want for me to go phone, Mas'r Grant?"

"No," said Alison. "If those two came back—"

"I don't think they will," Peter said. "Try to remember, darling. You fainted. When you came round this cousin of yours tried to get you to sign some paper or other giving him the estate and you refused."

"I told him it was a nonsense and wouldn't stand up in any court of law and anyway you were acting for me and would have to advise me and draw up anything I would sign."

"Good for you. What next?"

"He was angry but he just said all right we'd go back to Princeton. I said I would have to make the arrangements about Uncle Ben's funeral and the first thing was to get an undertaker. I said I would stay at Barrack Hill until the body was moved."

"That must have shaken them."

"It certainly did. They went into a huddle out here in the

hall. I was still in the bedroom. Dr Silver came back and said he would telephone to an undertaker in the morning. I said I was staying. They said in that case they would stay, too. I said I would be all right when Mrs Jackman came back. It was still quite early."

"It's not too terribly late yet," Peter assured her. "Go on."

"George went to the bar to fix some drinks for us while we waited. Pretty soon after that I must have passed out. I don't remember."

Jim, who was sitting near the main door got up suddenly, put down his empty glass and went outside. Peter got up too, but Alison caught his hand.

"Don't leave me," she whispered. "Not yet. I—I couldn't stand being alone."

He sat down again, putting an arm round her. Through the door that Jim had left open they saw a small car drive across the gravel and disappear round the corner of the house. Jim came in again.

"That Mistress Jackman," he said. "She's not know nothing. I think we not tell her too much, man."

A woman, middle-aged, stout, Fernandan, appeared at the half-open front door. Jim held it politely for her.

"And who are all of you people?" Mrs Jackman said, in a rich comfortable voice. "What are you doing in my hotel?"

Peter told her, simply saying that Miss Maclean, who was Colonel Wilberforce's niece, had received an urgent message to come to him because he was taken ill suddenly. Unfortunately she was too late.

Mrs Jackman showed signs of shock, but did not ask for any more details. Presently she said, "We knew his health was very bad. We knew he might have another heart attack any time."

"Another?" Alison asked.

"Last year. He said he had written to his sister in England to tell her."

Alison said nothing. Uncle Ben's letter had not mentioned

a definite heart attack; just a heart ailment more or less expected at his age.

Peter said, "I think we have met before, Mrs Jackman. You very kindly gave me a lift back to Princeton from Alamanda House this morning. I didn't want to wait for the minibus."

"Why, so we did," she said, quite unmoved by this further revelation. She added, politely, "I hope you were not late for your important appointment."

"We are wondering what to do now," Alison ventured, "because your telephone seems to be out of order. I expect the fire—"

"Fire!" she cried. "What have you been doing? What's this about fire?"

Peter hastened to explain what seemed to have happened at the back of the house. Jim added an account of how he had put out a fire, but Mrs Jackman was not appeased. She hurried away from the hall and they heard her exclaiming in anger and sorrow at the mess in her kitchen.

"More upset over her blasted stove than your poor old uncle," Peter said to Alison.

"Only it wasn't Uncle Ben," she answered. "I think you ought to have told her. Or perhaps she knows. Where on earth *is* Uncle Ben, anyway?"

Peter was about to suggest that, all things considered, he could not be far off, when Jim again strode to the door and flung it open. This time Alison got to her feet as Peter left his chair. Her legs were still shaky, but with his arm holding her they went forward to the threshold.

The drive was nearly filled by a large white ambulance. As it came to rest, two men jumped down from beside the driver. One was the ambulance attendant and the other was Inspector Vincent.

"How in the world—?" Peter was beginning, but Vincent guided him and Alison back into the house, after telling the ambulance crew to get their stretcher ready and bring it to the door, but wait there until he came back.

"Now," he said, turning to Peter. "Perhaps you'll explain, Mr Wilberforce, what all this is about."

"He isn't Mr Wilberforce," Alison protested. "He's Mr Peter Grant, my lawyer from England."

"Then where is Mr Wilberforce?"

"If you mean George Wilberforce, alias Gary Wilkins, cousin of Miss Maclean here, I don't know where he went after his car nearly put mine down the mountainside, leaving the drive here at about forty with a blind turn on to the road."

Inspector Vincent sighed. He was already tired of these eccentric Englishmen and their antics.

"I'll tell you what happened first," Alison said. "Then Peter can fill in with what he knows."

The inspector agreed, not expecting to find enlightenment. But at the end of it he jumped up briskly and demanded to see the body that had so far been identified only by Jim.

It was certainly Mr Gopal, he found. He had been killed by a rabbit punch in the same way as Manfred Stein. There was nothing to suggest where the murder had been committed or when or by whom, nor when and how the body had been brought to Barrack Hill.

"This Dr Silver, if he is a real doctor," Alison said, "was here when George brought me in his car. I thought it was Uncle Ben—"

"His face was covered by the mask," Peter said. "Jim took it off. He has it for you. It seems to have been taken from Superintendent Graham's room, so you'd better give it back to him."

The inspector nodded. The case was becoming clearer but it would have to be handled carefully if they were not to lose a murderer. So he explained what he had decided to do and explained how the others could help him. Then he left them in the hall while he went away to speak to Mrs Jackman and collect Jim who had gone to the kitchen to find something to eat, having missed his own meal at Gardenia Lodge. The recent excitements had given him a hearty appetite.

All this time the ambulance crew waited. They had put down the stretcher at the closed door of the hotel and after standing there for a few minutes had returned to the ambulance where they sat smoking thin cigars and talking in low voices. Waiting did not worry them, they rather enjoyed it. The air was cool in the mountains, the stars were bright, the glow in the sky to seaward was all they could see of Princeton from this point. Its glittering lights would come into view round the first bend on the homeward run, but the noise would not reach them until they passed Alamanda House.

When at last Inspector Vincent called them from the door they jumped down again, trod out their cigars on the pebbles and took their stretcher indoors. The sheeted figure on the bed was cold but not as stiff as they expected. How long had he been dead? Sometime that evening? And had grown so cold already?

"You are to take him to the hospital mortuary with this note," said Inspector Vincent. "You are then to take Miss Maclean and Mr Hulbert to the Gardenia Lodge Hotel."

"What about Peter?" Alison asked, fear and resentment in her voice.

"I'm staying on with the inspector for a bit," Peter said. "Then I can drive him back in my car."

He drew her into the now empty hall, away from the others. He put his arms round her and held her close.

"Only a little longer," he said gently. "Stick it out a little longer. We've got to get the thugs who tried to burn you."

"And who killed that poor Indian," she protested, but forgave him because he put her first, clinging to him, waiting for his kiss, content to be ruled at last.

When the ambulance had gone Mrs Jackman brought sandwiches and coffee to the two waiting men. Inspector Vincent told her to go to bed. There was no danger now, he explained.

"Then why do you stay?" she asked, still uncertain, still confused by all that had happened on this most mysterious evening.

"Because I think there will be a doubt in their minds," he answered. "You know who I mean?"

She nodded.

"They passed Mr Grant's car as they left here and they left in a hurry because they must have heard his car on the road. So I think Mr Wilkins or Wilberforce suffers uncertainty and will come back. We shall be most pleased to see him."

But it was not Gary Wilkins who returned. Just after midnight the watchers heard a labouring engine, some clashing gears, a further struggle. They went out into the drive, standing in the deep shadow of a larkspur tree.

A rickety van drew up near the door they had left deliberately half open. A tall man in a frock coat with a felt hat pulled down on his forehead got out slowly; his driver stayed behind the wheel.

Inspector Vincent stepped forward. Peter saw that he held a gun in his hand.

"Dr Silver," said Vincent, sharply, "what are you doing here? And why did you earlier desert your patient, Miss Maclean, leaving her in great danger?"

"I—we—were going for help, to arrange for the removal of the body—"

"Whose body?"

Dr Silver took a step back towards the van, one hand reaching behind him into the pocket of his tail coat.

Without hesitation Inspector Vincent fired, Dr Silver gave a yell of pain, the van driver started his engine and backed away jerkily, braking as he hit a tree and flinging himself from the driving seat into the undergrowth.

"Down!" the inspector shouted.

Peter obeyed him, but Vincent himself did not take cover. He flung himself at the big doctor, seized him by the collar of his coat, stripped it down and away and flung it far into the garden where it fell with a plop into the swimming pool and promptly sank out of sight.

Dr Silver, who was clutching his right arm and moaning, sank to his knees.

"Was that a gun or a grenade?" the inspector demanded sternly, making no effort to help his victim, who now showed signs of collapse.

He got no answer, so turned away, gun up again, to the empty van.

"You there!" he called. "Come out, man. If you had nothing to do with this come out and let me see who you are."

He came, cringing, protesting absolute ignorance. Dr Silver wanted his services as an undertaker. It was a private job for a young lady who wanted to arrange the funeral of her uncle. It was to be the next day, by cremation. The doctor had given a death certificate.

"You have that?"

"In my office, sah. To take to authorities in the morning."

"Good. You have been deceived. The arrangements have already been made. Your services will not be needed."

"But the bill? For this journey? For this—this—"

"Give me your name and address and get out. I will collect that certificate later tonight. See that you have it ready."

The undertaker, who, judging from the appearance of the van and his own scruffy clothes, was far from prosperous, did as he was ordered and promised to make a statement in confirmation of what he had said.

Peter left Dr Silver to Vincent and went into the house to find something to use as a bandage and sling. Mrs Jackman came out of the kitchen where she had been working to reduce the mess caused by the fire.

"A good thing I didn't take the inspector's advice and go to bed. What next, I wonder?" she said, when he asked her to help him.

"Nothing more, I hope," Peter assured her. "We'll be away now, very soon. But I don't want that brute's blood smearing my car."

They were away in five minutes, Inspector Vincent in the

back with Dr Silver nursing the flesh wound in his arm and Peter driving. At the police station the inspector and his prisoner got out. Peter drove on to the Marshalls' where he found the consul in a state of some excitement, waiting to hear his story. Certain news had come through to him, he explained. He wanted it confirmed by the man who had been on the spot. Peter was very willing to give his version of the night's events. He had thought of going to Gardenia Lodge to make sure that Alison was back there, safe and sound. But he told himself that nothing could have gone wrong since Jim was with her. The more he saw of Jim the more his admiration for the man had grown and was growing still.

CHAPTER THIRTEEN

But the day's work was not yet over for Peter. He had put his car away and was giving his name to the night porter at the consulate when a police car drew up at the curb. A young officer in plain clothes brought a message from Detective-Superintendent Graham. He would be much obliged if Mr Grant would go down to headquarters at once. Wearily, yawning, his eyes closing as they drove, Peter obeyed the summons.

He woke up with a jerk when the car stopped. There was no waiting; he was shown straight into Graham's room where a statement of all his movements, observations and conclusions since his arrival in San Fernando was taken down in writing and read over to him. He then signed it.

"Couldn't that have waited till the morning?" he asked, too tired to feel angry, longing only for a pillow to lay his head on, regardless of what happened to the rest of him.

"It could not wait," Graham said severely. "And it is already morning."

"I suppose so. Now what?"

Graham relented enough to apologise.

"But you see it is essential we have our case completely clear. From Dr Silver's confession—"

"Ah! That thug coughed up, did he?"

"Silver has never failed to attempt his own salvation at the expense of others. But the crooks rely on him when there is no one else. So far he has wriggled out of all trouble. Not so now. We will have him for a false death certificate and with luck as accessory after the fact of murder."

"Murder by George Wilberforce? Miss Maclean's cousin?"

"Her cousin, but his name *is* Gary Wilkins. He told her a lie when he pretended he used Wilkins for business purposes only. Of course his passport must be in his real name if it is to stand up to inquiry."

"Then when—?"

"He changed his name in the States. Or rather his mother changed it when she managed to settle there. She was taken in by her own family, who were American born and bred, when she went out with the boy. Gary Wilkins he was made and Gary Wilkins he stayed. His passport is OK. We've checked him with their Embassy."

"Where is he now? It was only Silver who came up in the undertaker's van. Why did *he* come, d'you think?"

"Probably Wilkins wanted to know what had happened. They meant the house to burn and the girl and the dead man with it. Then they could say they'd gone off at her request to get her uncle removed and she must have upset the stove in the kitchen while she was waiting and set the place on fire. Silver simply says he was asked to find an undertaker."

"Why did they plant all this at Barrack Hill, except that it's such an out of the way place?"

"Old Wilberforce owns it. I believe you already know that. He'd disappeared, so what more natural than that he'd been lying low there and then taken ill. Quite plausible."

"*Has* he been there?"

"What d'you think? How else could he get a message down

to us so we'd send up Inspector Vincent and an ambulance?"

"So that was it."

Radio communication. The old boy had some link with Security on this island, so the consul had hinted. Well, well. Send a message, but take no step whatever to rescue his niece!

"He couldn't do much more than he did," Graham said, rightly interpreting the expression on the young man's face. "He is genuinely ill, you know, Mr Grant."

Peter nodded. He did not want to betray his personal concern for Alison. Life at present was complicated enough without that.

"He dared not confront those two villains," Graham went on, "but he did what he could to control the fire until you got there and Jim helped him to put it out."

"Jim! Then he saw him! And never said a word. I suppose he knew he was there all the time?"

"Mr Grant," said Graham solemnly but with the brightness of suppressed laughter in his eyes, "I think there is very little about the retired Colonel Wilberforce that Jim Hulbert does not know. He is proud of his knowledge. That is why he was so overthrown by his one mistake over the body in the swimming pool."

Peter took this opportunity of escaping from any further talk at present of Alison's plight and narrow escape from death. It seemed her escape had not been so narrow after all. Her uncle would no doubt have saved her when the criminals left, whether he himself and Jim had arrived or not. He found this thought deflating. He changed the subject.

"Those three American buddies of this man, Wilkins? Where do they come into the picture? What's the big interest in the Barrack Hill estate anyhow?"

Superintendent Graham replied cautiously.

"I am not very clear on this, Mr Grant. I do know that they are not long-standing friends of Miss Maclean's cousin. They seem to have met at the airport, perhaps flew in on the same plane. That I do not yet know. They are business men, they belong to a big firm in the States promoting projects in foreign countries. Mr Forstal and Mr Bilton are surveyors, Forstal a geologist and Bilton a chemical engineer. Mr Leadbetter is some sort of business executive. I quote from their passports. I have no reason to question them—yet. So far they have behaved as tourists, only."

"As far as you know they have no connection with Gary Wilkins outside San Fernando?"

"None whatever."

After a moment's silence Graham leaned forward.

"I will now tell you, Mr Grant, of a little surprise I plan for Mr Wilkins tomorrow. You have a part in my plan which I will now tell you."

"Always supposing he hasn't scarpered already."

"Always supposing our controls at the harbour and airports and railway stations come up to scratch."

With that Peter had to be content. A police car took him back to the consulate, the night porter took him to his room and promised faithfully to call him again at six o'clock that morning, before he went off duty. It was then just after two.

At seven o'clock Alison woke from a deep sleep to the sound of repeated knocking at her door. Her first response was one of fear, a continuation of remembered terror. This fear had assailed her over and over again before she had slept at last with the dawn light filling her room. The sun was well up now, the air both stuffy and hot. Last night or whenever it was she had reached her room she had felt cold, chilled in mind and body and had switched off the air conditioning. Now she switched it on before stumbling from her bed.

Peter stood outside, smiling at her, though his face was still pale from the rigours of the day before.

"Can I come in?" he asked. "I've got to talk to you."

She stood aside for him, then locked the door again. When she turned from doing so he was just behind her, his arms ready to hold her close. She turned into them and leaned against him, her mind still clogged with sleep, but all the fear evaporated now in the joy of his nearness and the reality of their love.

Peter held her, cursing the circumstances that must spoil this encounter. Spoil it, curtail it, postpone 'the true end of love'. Only for a little while, he promised himself, not daring to kiss her as he longed to do, as he should do, feeling desire rising to overmaster him.

He said again, hoarsely, "I've got to talk to you, my darling."

Talk, good God, *talk!* But Graham had said there was still danger, so—

Alison felt his arms loosen. She loved him, she trusted him, she knew where their two thoughts had flown. Her Scottish blood gave her dignity.

"I'll dress," she said, moving to the inner door. Peter's instant shout of laughter restored them both. She grinned at him and disappeared. He heard the water begin to run in the shower.

He went out on to the verandah and sat down on a chair near her door. There had been no one in the drive when he arrived nor was there anyone to be seen there now. The door of the office was closed, the little verandah opposite empty, the door of the corridor shut. But from the kitchen came the sound of voices and the pleasant smell of bacon frying. Peter found his mind swimming, his head nodding. He slid down a little in the uncomfortable metal chair, pillowed his head on his arm and dozed.

"Here I am," said Alison brightly, leaning to plant a kiss on top of his now tousled hair. "What's the important talk about?"

He sat up with a jerk, narrowly missing her chin as he did so.

"If you'd butted me I'd have been out cold," she said reproachfully. "What about that talk?"

"Not out here," he said, catching at her hand to help him up.

They went back into her room. When they came out, walking hand in hand along the dark verandah to the back way into the dining room Alison had grasped the situation as far as

Peter could describe it and also knew what would happen that day and the part she had to play in it.

They were the first to arrive for breakfast. Jim guided them to a table near the window and offered them the old red leather-bound menu with his most professional gesture.

"Fruit juice, cornflakes, one egg, one strip of bacon, coffee toast and marmalade," Alison said, smiling up at him.

"Sounds fine. Me too," said Peter.

"Two eggs, two strips bacon?" Jim asked, grinning widely.

"Please."

"Hog," said Alison tenderly.

"Hog yourself! Bereaved too. You ought to be on dry toast and sedative."

"Incidentally," Alison said, looking serious. "What about clothes? This is hardly suitable, d'you think?"

'This' was lilac coloured slacks and an oatmeal, sleeveless loose top that made her auburn hair burn more brightly than ever round her pale face.

"It's entrancing," Peter said.

"For the ceremony," she reminded him. "It has to be a dress, I suppose? After all, it's Sunday, too, isn't it?"

"I can't advise. The loveliest thing I've seen was what you had on when I arrived this morning."

"I'm serious, Peter."

"So am I, my love. How desperately serious you have yet to—"

"Hush! Here they come!"

The three Americans could be heard laughing and talking in the corridor. Jim came through the kitchen door with two generous helpings of paw-paw.

"Better than that old orange juice," he said. "They been told, Missy Wilb," he added in a whisper.

The voices and laughter had stopped abruptly. Alison did not look up until she judged they were halfway across the floor. Then she lifted her head, transferred the handkerchief she held to her pocket and sent a sad smile in their direction.

"Don't ham it," Peter whispered, treading on her foot under the table.

"Ow!" she whispered back. "That's the second time you've ruined my toes!"

Ray Leadbetter came close, holding out a hand.

"May I say on behalf of my friends and myself how distressed we are to hear the sad news?"

"Yes," said Alison. "Thank you. We heard you all laughing in the corridor as you came in. Didn't we, Peter?"

"That was before Mr Mancini gave us the news," said Sam Forstal apologetically, but with an angry glint in his eyes.

"I'm sorry," Alison said, taking the handkerchief out again. "I'm upset. I didn't mean—"

Peter took the intended cue.

"Won't you people join us?" he said. "I'd like to tell you what happened. Alison would rather I did it for her, I know."

She nodded. Jim brought their cornflakes, took the paw-paw bowls, took orders from the others, retreated.

"I'm her lawyer, after all," Peter went on. "I'll be brief."

They smiled, acknowledging a fatuous joke he had not intended. Never mind. Let them think him a comic limey. It would do no harm.

"Well, the gist of it is Alison didn't know her uncle owned Barrack Hill, nor that he was there when we went up yesterday morning. But he got in touch with me later and I went up. I found he'd been taken ill and a doctor had been sent for. This was after the two girls who worked there had left. The house-keeper was having a day off."

"D'you mean Olive and Jean? Gary brought them along here to dine."

"I got on to the office here to tell Alison to come out directly," Peter said blandly.

Alison blew her nose and hung her head to hide her mirth at the bare-faced lie.

"Don't go on," Ray said. "You're distressing Alison. We

needn't hear any more. Gary took Alison along and you were too late—I mean, your uncle had already passed on."

Jim brought cornflakes for the newcomers and coffee, toast, marmalade, bacon and eggs for the bereaved and her adviser. The Americans exchanged glances of wonder, even incredulity. British phlegm. Easier perhaps for others to cope with than the conventional hysteria. But *no*, revolting, unwomanly, un-American—

Alison put away the unsoaked handkerchief and poured coffee.

"Peter was a great help," she said quietly. "He arranged everything. The ambulance brought me back and took poor Uncle Ben—on."

"The funeral will be this afternoon," Peter said, beginning to attack his bacon and eggs with spirit. "But the coffin will come here first for a short lying-in before going to the crematorium. We shall take the ashes to England."

Alison nodded.

"My mother," she said and left it at that. "We thought, as Mr Wilberforce had lived here for over a year—here and up at Barrack Hill— He used to go there for the summer, cooler, of course and came down here in the winter while the tourist season was on. Warmer and quieter, you know."

The three laughed aloud at this intended, but simple joke. Peter smiled bleakly, Alison looked severe.

"Anyway the staff here appreciated him," Peter said. "I'm sure Alison would like me to invite you three to join us in the lounge at noon. You never met the old gentleman, but as you are staying here and know his nephew, Gary Wilkins—"

"Nephew," said Sam thoughtfully. "But not Alison's brother."

"Her cousin."

"Another sister of Mr Wilberforce?"

"No. He had only one sister and one brother."

"Then how come?"

Peter smiled politely.

"Gary Wilkins's mother changed her name from Wilberforce to Wilkins when she went back to live with her parents in the US. So the boy's name was changed, too."

Ray sent a questioning glance at Peter, but the latter was now spreading marmalade on a piece of toast and did not look up.

The Mancinis came in to their table near the kitchen door and took their places without making their usual bows to their guests. They were very seriously put out by the arrangements Inspector Vincent had ordered them to make. A lying-in-state for that shabby old man, who might be a murderer and who had cheated them of their insurance money by dying a natural death, according to the certificate of Dr Silver.

"That Dr Silver!" Mrs Mancini said with great indignation. "How dare he break his word with us that there would be an accident certified?"

"He is a cheat and a criminal," said Mr Mancini. "And keep your voice down, Maria. That English lawyer is looking at you. I will never use Dr Silver again."

"Has the insurance refused to pay?"

"Naturally it has refused to pay. No accident, no claim. It is worse than that. I have a letter, by messenger—came just now —to say cause of death stated means deceased was suffering from heart disease already and not in good health as stated by me with certificate from Dr Silver. So all insurance cancelled."

"Didn't I tell you," Mrs Mancini said, bitterly, "to wait and not to risk this accident policy? He is old and ill. Insurance for natural death would have given us the money."

"You fool woman!" Mancini hissed at her. "They would not give policy for old, sick man. Or only with premium sky high."

He waved an arm, nearly knocking over his coffee cup.

"I will send Paula for some lilies," Mrs Mancini said. "I will not have a coffin in my lounge without flowers."

"Then put the price on Miss Maclean's bill."

"It is you is a fool, Luigi," she said, with contempt. "What else would I do?"

Gary Wilkins drove into the Gardenia Lodge Hotel just after eleven that morning. He had spent most of the time since the night before trying to discover what had happened at Barrack Hill after he had left in such a hurry. Had his plan succeeded or failed miserably? Silver ought to have reported but his phone was dead. Silver had promised to report when he got back with the undertaker. He had not even told him the name far less the address of this ally. Now he had disappeared. The newspapers were silent, too. A conspiracy of silence? He shivered at the thought. But he was obstinate and greedy as well as stupid. He had a potential deal with the Leadbetter lot. He was determined to see it through, somehow.

In this state of half jitters Gary mounted the drive at Gardenia Lodge in low gear. Turning the corner at the top he saw in front of him a State ambulance from which at that moment two men were carefully drawing out a long closed coffin, to bear into the house.

For a second he thought of turning and driving away, to the harbour, to the airfield, even to the mountains. But another car was now moving up the steep drive. A black car with a uniformed driver at the wheel. Gary drew into the side to give the black car room to pass. But it nosed in close behind Gary. With the ambulance in front he was now very neatly boxed in.

He got out and locked his car door. Superintendent Graham and Inspector Vincent got out of the police car. He knew their action was deliberate; they must have followed him all the way. He had not noticed them because their car was not marked. He knew that they intended him to understand their action. Without hesitation he walked up to them.

"My name is Wilkins," he said. "Gary Wilkins. I am the late Mr Wilberforce's nephew. Is there something you want to tell me?"

CHAPTER FOURTEEN

Superintendent Graham gave him a slow smile.

"There's several things I have to tell you," he said. "But there's a good deal you have to tell me, first."

He looked about him. The drive seemed to be filling up with people. The Mancinis had appeared on the verandah beside their room; two maids with brooms were crossing from the kitchen to the guests' verandah. The office door was open; Paula, in a short red and orange dress with a high collar, stood just inside it, watching.

Graham decided not to continue the interview in such a public spot. He thought of the swimming pool and smiled again. There might be an interesting reaction at the swimming pool. Or, of course, there might not. But it would be hidden from curious eyes; it would be quiet. He turned to Inspector Vincent and nodded.

"Be ready at noon," he said. "Ah, here is Jim Hulbert. All correct, Jim?"

"Yes, Superintendent sah."

"Then we will have a little chat," Graham said to Gary Wilkins. "Come with me."

Leaning into the police car he spoke a few words to the driver. Then turning again he began to move away, Gary walking most unwillingly beside him.

Contrary to the superintendent's expectation, the swimming pool was already occupied. Sitting on the shady side were the three Americans, Peter and Alison. Gary made a sharp movement when he caught sight of them, but Graham, who had seen them a second before, dropped back a step and his hand went to his pocket.

"Well," he said, quietly. "Perhaps my questions and yours will be answered together."

Gary was welcomed, without enthusiasm, by his three friends, who left him to find himself a chair. Peter on the other hand jumped up to give his to the superintendent and sat down at Alison's feet. For a little while after Graham was introduced and they were all settled again no one spoke. Then Ray said, "Lieutenant, or is it Captain, we still are not quite clear what's been going on at Barrack Hill overnight. My friends and I have an interest—"

"Which is?" asked Graham politely.

"The coffee estate and hotel belonging to Mr Wilberforce, a client of my firm in London," Peter said, sharply. "These gentlemen want to buy it. The first question is who they should approach, Mr Wilberforce being—er—absent."

"The question as I see it," said Sam Forstal, "is who the property now belongs to. Gary, here, gave us to understand he was a nephew, son of an elder brother, and had a prior claim."

"And had come out from the States to persuade his uncle to sell out to him," Ray continued the tale. "But he doesn't seem to have got all that far, since the old man disappeared the day after Gary saw him and has since died."

"So we need to know who is the heir," Chester Bilton said. "If there was a will."

"There was a will," Graham told them. "I have passed my copy on to Mr Grant, as the representative of the family firm of lawyers. The original is with the bank."

"Then why the hell was I not told?" Gary burst out furiously. He had been sitting forward, white-faced, tense, during his friends' rather slow deliberate remarks, but this evidently took him by surprise. "I don't think much of our family lawyer if he can't keep me informed of what passes."

"Chiefly because you didn't choose to inform us, when you came to London, calling yourself George Wilberforce, that you intended to come out here and try to persuade your uncle to give or sell you his estate, which, together with Barrack Hill Hotel, forms his sole capital asset. You made it very clear to my firm that all you want is money and that you are not particular how you come by it."

Gary's face had turned scarlet now with anger, but he forced himself to speak quietly.

"You say you have a will. Who made it?"

"Your uncle, of course. He signed it before witnesses on the evening of the day after you came to see him. His Indian lawyer here in Princeton sent a copy by special messenger to Superintendent Graham."

The superintendent nodded, watching Gary very closely. The latter had conquered his rage; his face had grown still and sullen, a defence he had probably formed in childhood and used, despite its futility, ever since.

A silence fell on the gathering, broken a little later by Ray Leadbetter.

"Well then," he said in a friendly voice, "that seems to be that. No more mystery, is there? Mr Grant—Peter—will tell us who we need to deal with and—"

"If the estate is mine or Alison sells it to me, I'll deal with you three," Gary broke in obstinately. "Otherwise nothing doing as far as I'm concerned."

"Does anything at all have to be doing with you, Gary?" Sam asked gently. "I mean to say, we three might decide to deal primarily with Miss Maclean."

"Peter would deal for me," said Alison. "Or rather I expect it would be with my mother. She is the real heir, isn't she, Peter, though I believe the estate is in trust for me, whatever that means. I don't think we could get as far as doing an actual deal, naming a price, just like that, off the cuff."

The Americans looked at her with approval. Gary scowled as he had when he noticed Peter's tie on the ground the afternoon before, very near to where they were all sitting now. Superintendent Graham continued to watch Gary.

Peter said, "I don't think we can get any further at all at present. I can tell you that the will that was passed to me was drawn up quite recently and signed and dated only two nights ago and that it appears perfectly authentic. It would be easier if Mr Henry Gopal was able to tell us the circumstances in which he received instructions from Mr Wilberforce for this will and in which it was signed. But that, unfortunately, is not possible."

"Why not?" asked Chester.

"I tried to contact him two days ago," Alison told him. "But he wasn't at his office, which is also his house. So I went to see the Superintendent here."

"That is correct," said Graham, with such finality that no one dared to ask for the lawyer's present whereabouts.

"This will," said Peter, continuing his explanation, "has to be proved and probate obtained for acting upon its provisions. In England this process takes about six months."

The three Americans looked grave.

"You could tell us *why* you want to buy Uncle Ben's coffee estate," Alison said. It was an important point and one that had puzzled her from the moment she heard of their purpose. "Because," she added, "I don't suppose it's coffee and if it's archaeology, something you want to dig up, remains of ancient civilisations—well, won't you have to get this government's approval? We shall have to consult experts, shan't we, Peter?"

"There are no remains of value behind the Spanish occupation," Graham said severely. "But we have valuable deposits of minerals. You have seen our bauxite works, Miss Maclean? On your way from the airport?"

"I came by ship," she answered. "What is bauxite?"

The Americans looked depressed. No one answered her questions. Peter made a note on an envelope. As a wife Alison would be quite a challenge, he thought, with pleasure rather than misgiving.

Gary, though he stayed where he was, withdrew his thoughts from this infuriating set of mugs, as he considered them. The situation was serious. His first impulse the night before, when his brilliant plan had been interrupted by the bloody young busybody, Grant, was to scuttle, make for the nearest airport, drop everything, pick up his bag on the way and get out on any plane that could give him a seat. That impulse had been correct. It was that damned witch doctor, Silver, who had stopped him. Play it cool, Silver had advised. The girl was bound to be confused if she did not die, Silver insisted. She might already be suffocated by the smoke from the fire. He himself had guessed it was Grant in the car that nearly crashed him in the drive as he drove out. He should have pushed him off the road. Again it was Silver whose warning shout knocked him off balance so that he automatically avoided contact instead of making sure of it.

Well then, what had Grant found? A fire to fight, a girl unconscious to bring round, a corpse in a bed, wearing the mask of Uncle Ben with a death certificate on the table made out and signed by Silver.

A corpse. Was it really possible Grant had not discovered the truth about that stiff? Just possible, but very unlikely.

Silver had not let him down any further. He had dropped the old crook near the house of an undertaker he said would work for him. He had gone back to his cheap lodgings near the harbour and waited. No news of any kind. This morning early he had gone to that street and by asking questions had found the undertaker, a man of Chinese extraction, who was in a state of great fear and indignation.

"I go with hearse and coffin," the man had said. "There is no sick girl, no dead man. Only the head of CID and a young man. They take Dr Silver for long talk, then come out and send me away. Who pays my bill? Where is the doctor?"

It had been easy to promise him payment later, impossible to find out where Silver was. Gone to earth, most likely, if he was free. Unless he was still being held, for more questioning. He had a record. He had even confessed to it when the job was put to him. But greedy, as they all were, Gary told himself bitterly. It did not occur to him that his own greed had begun this chain of ill-luck. And his own stupidity, reflecting and strengthening the greed.

The undertaker had one important piece of news, though. A police ambulance had been at Barrack Hill and had taken away Mr Wilberforce, probably the girl too, though they did not tell him so. He had heard through contacts, he said vaguely, that Mr Wilberforce was to be buried that afternoon but the coffin would go to Gardenia Lodge first, since that had been where he had spent most of the last months of his life.

A coffin. A state ambulance. He had seen it. Was it possible the mask had deceived them all, the death certificate also?

In acute agony of mind Gary told himself this too was possible, but very very unlikely. So he was in a trap. He had driven into it of his own accord, to find the ambulance unloading, blocking the drive in front of him and the police car immediately after, just behind, blocking his rear.

At other times, in other ploys, a well-managed job. He dared not even put a hand to his pocket for he knew Graham's eyes were still fixed on him and down in the drive there were the uniformed bastards, arms at the ready, he was sure.

Superintendent Graham looked at his watch. Peter looked at his watch. Ray Leadbetter looked at his watch.

"I think," said Peter smoothly, "speaking on behalf of Miss Maclean and the family, it is time we went in for our short ceremony. Perhaps you will all follow us."

He got up, gave his hand to Alison and walking slowly beside her led the way from the swimming pool. The Americans were a little awed by the formality and coldness of the chief mourners but they respected ritual. They even accepted Gary into their ranks, though their general attitude towards him was markedly less cordial than heretofore.

The staff of the hotel, together with the Mancinis, was already assembled in the drive. Inspector Vincent, with the crews of the ambulance and police car had placed themselves outside this group, unostentatiously surrounding it.

Gary saw that he was moving still further into the trap, if such it was. He had one desperate impulse to break away, but thought better of it. Superintendent Graham was joining the procession to the lounge where the lying-in was to take place, but Vincent and the others were in the drive. Also his car was still boxed in. The ambulance seemed to have taken over the role of hearse.

Jim, hovering near the corridor to the lounge, stepped forward when he saw the party approaching from the swimming pool and drew Peter to one side. A brief discussion took place, Jim explaining, Peter agitated, protesting. When he returned to Alison's side he took her hand again, drew her close to him and whispered, "Be prepared for a shock, darling."

She whispered back, "Are they going to arrest him?"

"I hope so."

"Where's the chaplain?"

He shrugged. He had done his best. It would be less sacrilegious if the chaplain was late or did not turn up at all. This came of Graham's exuberant sense of melodrama. Hateful, but it would soon be over. He had a thought for Gary, but not of compassion.

Peter with Alison leading, followed closely by the Mancinis, the procession moved in pairs along the corridor to the lounge and went in. The coffin lay on trestles at the far end where the television normally stood. The door into the dining room was closed, a curtain hung over the opening to the verandah. It was not possible to see if the barred glass door there, which at night was padlocked, had also been secured. The usual half light filtered through the thin window curtains. One electric bulb, shaded, cast a subdued beam down upon the coffin, from which the lid had been removed.

When everyone had entered the lounge and stood clustered near the corridor Peter and Alison moved forward alone, bowed their heads, looked into the open coffin and moved to the foot of it where they stood together, waiting.

Alison's face had grown white; she was trembling violently.

"They've put on the mask again," she whispered to Peter.

"Hush! I warned you. Hang on!"

The Mancinis came, bowed their heads, peered into the coffin, crossed themselves and went back to their places at the end of the room. The staff followed. The Americans came behind them with pained faces, observing this barbaric local custom as they thought it, resenting the fact that no one had warned them of the ordeal. Gary Wilkins came last with Superintendent Graham at his heels.

Throughout this ritual Alison had stood, shocked, terrified of the expected sequel. The dead man's face alone was visible, a decent white shroud covering him to the chin. Mrs Mancini's sheaf of lilies lay on his chest. Surely, as a Hindu—or had he been a Parsee—this masquerade was blasphemous, she thought. There must be some other way of frightening her evil cousin into confession.

There was. Gary had steeled himself to follow the performance of the others. He saw the mask, which he knew from the behaviour of the others must be in place, he bowed his head as they had done and then stared again at that remarkable facsimile. Two pale eyes stared back at him; the blue lips parted in a grim smile.

Gary's cry of horror was immediately echoed by the shrieks of everyone present as Mr Wilberforce, shaking off his shroud, sat up in the coffin. The lilies scattered, the Fernandans present, moaning their prolonged terror, sank on their knees and from there to their faces on the floor. The Mancinis held one another up, chattering with fright. Peter put an arm round Alison.

The Americans reeled back, snatching at their handkerchiefs to mop their faces on which a cold sweat had broken out. Even Graham was shaken; this development was totally unexpected. Only Jim and his wife Therese remained calm, standing just inside the dining room door which Jim had now opened, anticipating a need for water to revive the weaker souls.

"Well, George," Mr Wilberforce said. "You've made a proper mess of it, haven't you?"

Before the murderer could pull himself together or the superintendent recover from his surprise Paula, who had remained on her knees staring at the risen corpse, now screamed out, "That man Wilkins he make me do it! He make me send message! He make me take money! Not my fault. He make me! Each time he come he promise—he prom—"

She flung up her arms, overbalanced and fell on her face in a faint.

CHAPTER FIFTEEN

There was pandemonium in the darkened lounge. After their first paralysis of fear the Fernandan staff got trembling to their feet again. They had seen Peter Grant help the lean, bowed figure from the coffin. They had seen that he was wearing his usual shabby clothes but without his old grey cardigan. Zombie he might be. They were not convinced the Mas'r Wilb they had known, with his shuffling gait and whispering voice, had not been supernatural from the start. But the bolder spirits among them were reassured by his familiar appearance and a little ashamed to notice Therese's open contempt for them and Jim's genial pity.

Superintendent Graham was so ashamed of his own initial fright that he could think of nothing but a display of force. He called loudly for Vincent who was guarding the outer door into the corridor. He ordered Jim to shut and lock the dining room door from the lounge. When his police reinforcements arrived he ordered them to clear the room of the hotel staff with the exception of Paula, who had by now recovered from her faint and was lying back in an armchair with her eyes closed. Gary Wilkins, still stunned by the preposterous reappearance of his uncle, remained standing at the centre of the small family group, his face blank, his thoughts whirling. Nobody took any notice of the three Americans, who had moved quietly to the door on to the verandah, first to switch aside the curtains and then to stand in a row, blocking the entrance.

Inspector Vincent walked across to Graham's side to speak to him in a low voice. The superintendent nodded, waited a moment, then spoke.

"When I authorised this—this so-called ceremony," he began, "I did so after I had visited the hospital, where last night a body recovered from the Barrack Hill Hotel was examined and found to be dead, the neck having been broken in the same manner as that of a certain Manfred Stein, found here in the swimming pool three days ago."

Only three days, Alison realised with astonishment. It felt now like three months, three years.

"This body at Barrack Hill, when Miss Maclean was shown it by a certain Dr Silver, purported to be that of Mr Wilberforce here. It was wearing a mask that had been found covering the head of Manfred Stein and that was held in my safe keeping until yesterday when it was stolen from my room at police headquarters."

"Paula!" Alison exclaimed. "I remember now. I saw someone going into your room, Superintendent. As I left you on the steps of the police station. I thought then that I knew the back, but the dress was different from the one she'd had on in the morning."

Her explanation was cut short by Paula, who moaned aloud, "He make me go. He make me do it. I was so frightened, but he make me."

"Shut up!" said Graham fiercely. "You good for nothing trash! Who made you, who gave this order? You came about your register and the passports. Mr Mancini has always sent you. How much money did you get for this? This stealing?"

Paula hid her face in her hands and sobbed loudly.

Mr Wilberforce said, in a rather louder voice than usual, "My nephew's plan was simple and might have succeeded if my niece had not shown unusual intelligence. When Paula gave the false message—another fat reward, eh, Paula?—to Alison, and George here nobly volunteered to drive her out to Barrack

Hill, she managed to tell Jim where she was going and he told Peter and they went off together as soon as Jim was free. So the second phase of nephew George's little plan did not come off, thanks to their arrival."

Gary Wilkins roused himself at last. They were discussing him, describing the whole affair as if he was not there among them. His position was desperate really, but that did not excuse—

"You're very glib with your guesses," he said loudly, roughly. "What little plan?"

"The fire," said Uncle Ben. "The fire that was to kill Alison who had been drugged. And also to destroy any identification of the dead man. A good idea but poorly carried out."

"Rot!" shouted George, anger now mastering him. "Bloody, stinking rot! You can't prove a thing! How d'you suppose *you* know what happened last night? Fairy tale! Alison asked me to make arrangements for her uncle's funeral, to get an undertaker to go to Barrack Hill. She insisted on staying there with the dead man. We couldn't persuade her to leave. She must have knocked over something in the kitchen to start that fire and then was overcome by the smoke and—"

"How did you know the fire started in the kitchen?" Graham demanded.

"How does *he* know?" yelled Gary, now beside himself with rage. "Ask him that! Ask him who the body was, ask him when he put it there! Ask him how he killed his lawyer Gopal and why!"

The strident voice, the pointing, stabbing finger brought all eyes round to Mr Wilberforce, whose cold eyes stared back at his nephew as they had from the coffin, accusing, compelling.

"I know these things because I saw them happen," the old man said. "I was at Barrack Hill all the time. All the time, that is to say, after I had been with Henry Gopal to sign my will, suggest that he send it by messenger to Superintendent Graham, and warn him to be on his guard against you, George. I'm afraid he cannot have taken me seriously."

Superintendent Graham had listened to these exchanges with marked impatience. The confrontation he had allowed, though with some misgiving, had misfired. Or had Security gone over his head to alter it? Vincent had just told him where Gopal's body now was. He intended to carry out what he had originally planned should take place at the hospital.

"That's enough!" he shouted, laying a heavy hand on Gary's shoulder. "You will all come with me to Mr Wilberforce's room. Then we will see which is the guilty man, which has had the strength to strike the blows, the identical blows, to kill. This way, man. We go first."

"The hell we do!" screamed Gary, fear now riding his fury. He twisted away from Graham's hand, shot across the room to the verandah door, floored Chester Bilton, dived between his falling body and Ray Leadbetter, scrambled up and darted away over the lawn.

Inspector Vincent had his gun out and fired at the moment Chester fell with Gary beside him. The bullet sang through the gap above their bodies and smacked into one of the pillars of the verandah. Ray and Sam had dropped the second they saw Vincent's hand go up, so no one was hit. The inspector leaped over the prostrate bodies, firing another shot at the flying figure as it jumped into the cover of the drive. He ran out to the road in pursuit, but it was too late. A small crowd was collecting there, having heard the shots and recognised them for what they were. Gary was nowhere to be seen. Inspector Vincent told the people sternly to disperse and went back to the lounge.

Meanwhile Superintendent Graham had rushed away to telephone and the three Americans, getting up from the floor, rather sheepishly and shakily went over to the remaining three, still standing near the empty coffin.

"Sorry," Ray said, to no one in particular. "That took us rather by surprise. We should have held him."

"You did very well, very smartly," said Uncle Ben, smiling for the first time. "I congratulate you. Also I am obliged to you.

I was not looking forward to seeing George arrested in front of me. Murderer he may be, is in fact, but he is also my nephew."

This seemed to remind him of something. He turned to Alison, who was regarding him with undisguised horror.

"I'm so sorry, my dear," he whispered, "that I was not here to greet you when you arrived. I do apologise."

He held out both hands to her.

"I know it's been a long time. You were barely out of the nursery. Have you forgotten your old uncle?"

Alison gave a little cry, turned from him, collapsed into Peter's arms and burst into loud sobs.

The Americans tiptoed away. Mr Wilberforce sat down in an armchair near to the one where Paula still lay, apparently unable to recover sufficiently to get to her feet and go to her office.

"Paula," said Mr Wilberforce, softly, "how much did George give you?"

She stiffened, screwed her eyelids more tightly shut, pressed her lips together.

"I would like you to give that money to the box for blind children you have on the counter in the office," Mr Wilberforce went on. "Then I can say to Superintendent Graham that you were out of your mind just now and you have no money, so he will not send you to prison."

"Yes, sir," Paula gasped, seeing some hope of avoiding immediate arrest.

"I will watch you put this money in the box, Paula," said Mr Wilberforce. "And then I will take the key away until the box can be emptied."

She moaned, but after an inward struggle she said, "Yes, sir," again and sat up and dried her eyes with both hands.

Mr Wilberforce looked at Jim, who was still standing beside the dining room door. Jim unlocked the door to let Paula go through, then slipped out himself.

Graham came back, striding importantly.

"He can't get off the island, you know," he said loudly, as

if to convince himself of this. "The airports were warned last night and the harbour. We've doubled the warning and the guards. He won't try anything, you know, before dark."

"I should hope not," whispered Mr Wilberforce from his armchair.

The superintendent glanced at Peter. He was sitting near the open entrance to the verandah with Alison beside him. She had turned her chair to the opening to see the light and get the air, but it flowed over her hot and dry, though the verandah was in shade.

"I would like you, Mr Wilberforce, to come with me to your room and Mr Grant also. Miss Maclean would perhaps like to go to her own room."

"Thank you," said Alison in a shaky voice that spoke of more tears, "but I think I'll stay here."

The three men moved away, leaving her to her memories of a very different Uncle Ben from the shambling, horrifying figure of this morning. She gazed sadly at the humming birds darting among the hibiscus flowers and wished with her whole heart that she had never come to this place.

In Mr Wilberforce's room the sheeted figure of Henry Gopal lay on the bed where Jim had placed it when the substitution had been made.

"My fault, not Jim's," Mr Wilberforce insisted, seeing Graham's face darken with anger. "I told him to get the ambulance crew to put the coffin in here and leave him to arrange the corpse for viewing. As good Fernandans and good Catholics they did what he asked. Waited outside and then carried me into the lounge, lilies and all. They didn't seem to notice the difference in weight."

He smiled gently but the superintendent was not amused.

"I came back of course from Barrack Hill during the night," Mr Wilberforce explained.

"Why did you go up there at all?" asked Graham. "We are going to charge Wilkins with this murder." He pointed to the bed. "We have still to hear what happened to Manfred Stein."

"Yes." Mr Wilberforce was quite serious now. "I left him after a second short talk standing beside the swimming pool on Wednesday afternoon, I found him, dead, in a cubicle there when I went up for my evening bathe."

Graham nodded.

"Jim has told me of the usual routine, you know."

"It would have been my turn next," Mr Wilberforce went on. "I had to have time. So I had to act at once. I sent Jim with a note to Gopal telling him to send my new will, that I'd signed only that day, to you and to the bank for safe keeping. I had to clear out at once. Poor Henry, he obeyed the first of these instructions, but not the second."

"I saw him after Stein was found. He told me very little. He could have asked for protection."

The old man looked at Graham thoughtfully. He knew all about the racial antagonism. He knew that Gopal was too proud to appeal for help and Graham too unsympathetic to offer it.

"I went back to the swimming pool when I had sent Jim off with a note," he said. "I undressed Stein and put him into my own bathing trunks. I put my mask on his head, pulled him out of the cubicle and dropped him into the water. I let down the lilo and sank it. I put on Stein's clothes, left my dressing gown and towel in the cubicle, collected money and a few papers from my room and made my way to Barrack Hill where I stayed in hiding until last night or rather early this morning."

"So they knew at Barrack Hill that you were there?" Peter said.

"Only Mrs Jackman. The girls didn't know. They don't live in. We guessed when George invited the girls out he had some scheme on. I think he must have got the hotel keys from one of them. So I sent Mrs Jackman away for the day and kept watch myself. My nephew is not very clever, you may have noticed. Not at all like his father."

Again he smiled a bitter little smile that deepened the lines of his ancient face.

Graham said, "You pulled that man from the cubicle to the water? You were told your heart was bad, very bad, a danger of sudden death."

"Yes, I was. I preferred the risk to having a rabbit punch from young George."

Wheels ground on the gravel outside. Mr Wilberforce got up to look out of his window.

"It's the hearse," he said. "And the Gopal family clan. We must have the coffin back in here. I'll go out to speak to them. The coroner has made an order for burial, I believe?"

"At the hospital last night."

Peter got up, too. Jim came knocking at the door, crying, "Mas'r Wilb, Mas'r Wilb, they'se come take Mas'r Gopal! I go fetch coffin, Mas'r Wilb?"

"I'll help you, Jim," Peter said, joining him in the corridor.

They had not taken more than one step in the direction of the lounge when they heard a scream, the sound of falling furniture, a loud bang, a cry for help.

"Alison!" shouted Peter, leaping forward.

The girl had grown slowly calmer as the minutes passed after the men had left her. She told herself that poor Uncle Ben was old, perhaps a bit round the bend, at any rate not the attacker but the attacked. With a bad heart, too. She could have been more tolerant. All the same, he could have warned her and it had been a shock, a truly hideous shock.

She had reached this equilibrium of mind and recovered her full physical strength when she saw the roof of the hearse, decorated with black plumes, move into the drive. She jumped up to see it better, heard a sound behind her and turned. Paula stood there, a small bared knife in her hand.

Alison moved quickly. She had been an athletic child, playing most games easily and well. She had played in her school teams and at her university. She was quite ready to defend herself now. She seized the arms of the chair she had been sitting in and pushed it hard at Paula. As the dark girl reeled to keep her balance Alison leaped past her. Paula brought the knife down at her but missed. Alison shot behind the trestles, the empty coffin between herself and the enemy. The scream that startled the men in the corridor came from Paula, baulked for the moment of her revenge. In her mind Gary's failure was Alison's fault. The red-haired, long-legged, white-faced bitch had used witchcraft at Barrack Hill. Why else should Gary fail? Why was he on the run, leaving her behind, when he'd promised her—he'd promised—

Blind and stupid with anger and fear Paula rushed forward, regardless of the obstacle between her and her target. She lifted her arm to throw the knife. Alison tipped up the coffin as a shield, pushed it too hard. It turned over and fell, carrying Paula with it, shutting her underneath, pinning her to the floor. Alison yelled for help.

The two men stopped dead at the door of the lounge. Alison, clutching one of the trestles, trying to recover her breath, panted, "Paula! Tried to knife me! She's under—under—"

Jim gave a hoarse cry, running forward. He flung back the coffin. Paula lay there, crumpled, twisted. Her face was blue and swollen, her right hand still held the little knife which was plunged deep into her own right thigh.

Peter stooped over her, then looked up with a white face. "She's dead!" he cried. "She can't have been underneath for more than a few seconds! Alison, what happened? What *happened*, my darling?"

She shook her head. This was too much, too much. There was nothing to say, it was all madness, unreal, a nightmare returned yet again.

"Don't touch that knife, Peter!"

Mr Wilberforce was there, on his knees beside the dead girl, pushing Peter away, unclasping the dead fingers from the hilt of the knife. Very carefully he drew it out, holding it at arm's length, point down over the body as he turned his head to Graham who was just behind him.

"All yours, Superintendent," he said, "Have you anything really safe to put this in?"

"She can't be dead!" Alison moaned. "I tipped the thing up only a minute before they came in. She can't have been suffocated in a few *seconds*!"

"She wasn't suffocated at all," Uncle Ben said, looking up at her with kindly concern. "You've nothing to blame yourself for. She was killed by her own knife, poisoned ready for you, my dear. The coffin drove her arm down, that's all."

This time Alison allowed herself to be taken to her room and this time Peter stayed with her. Neither of them felt like eating lunch in the dining room, but when later on Jim came knocking at the door Peter accepted the tray he brought and put it down on the dressing table. Alison turned away from it but was persuaded to eat a little sliced mango. Peter tried something more solid but soon gave up.

Alison, thoroughly exhausted by the excitement of the last two days, slept in the afternoon while Peter went to find Mr Wilberforce. The latter was also taking a siesta but Jim was still about, cleaning the lounge carpet where Paula's blood had spilled.

"You oughtn't to be doing this," Peter told him.

"Nobody else, man," Jim said cheerfully. "Too much fright. Poison very very strong, you know. Little bit scratch on hand —pouf! All say they have scratch."

He laughed good-naturedly and got to his feet.

"No more poison," he said. "That silly girl! Big money, she wants, you know. Big money from that poor crazy killer—"

He shook his head. Peter looked round the room. The trestles had gone. The television set was back in place, the armchairs in their usual positions.

"Gopal relations take him away just in shroud," Jim said, answering Peter's unspoken question. "So they put Paula in that coffin with the lid on, you know, and go back in ambulance to hospital."

Another postmortem, another inquest. Where would it end? Peter went out wearily to his car. They would tell him the latest news at the consulate. In the meantime, sleep. As he drove away he remembered that he had not yet found time or opportunity to ask Alison to marry him.

CHAPTER SIXTEEN

Peter too slept soundly that afternoon. Though he had given orders to wake him about five, these were countermanded by the consul. He woke to find the world in darkness and Mr Marshall at his bedside, having just switched on the table lamp.

"I said five," Peter complained, throwing off the sheet and sitting up.

"I said leave you sleeping," the other answered, calmly. "There was nothing for you to do and you needed rest."

"What's the time, then?"

"Just seven. Dinner at the Gardenia is at seven-thirty or thereabouts. Colonel Wilberforce hopes you and his niece will join him there."

Peter ran his hands through his hair and dropped his legs over the side of the bed, his thoughts upon an immediate shower.

"If Alison's agreeable—" he began, snatching at a towel, but the consul was already closing the door behind him.

Alison was agreeable, if rather subdued. She had slept very deeply and had been wakened by Therese, sent by Jim to convey Uncle Ben's invitation. She showered and dressed quickly, determined to present herself to her uncle as a less hysterical spectacle than she had been during that first fantastic meeting which now seemed to have happened in another world in another century of time.

She found Uncle Ben sitting on the verandah outside the lounge. Jim had rigged a few coloured lights on the remains of the lattice between the pillars, so the place was not dark but softly illuminated.

Uncle Ben was sitting in his usual wicker chair. On the table beside him there was an old-fashioned cut glass decanter of sherry and three glasses. As the girl stepped out of the lounge the old man got to his feet. She saw that he was wearing a suit of faded shantung silk with a shirt and tie. Moved by this effort on his part she went up to him, kissed his cheek and said, "I'm sorry I behaved so shockingly badly this morning, Uncle Ben. Not even to say thank you for last night! I think you saved my life. Perhaps Peter's too."

"You should thank Jim," the old man said, gruffly, sitting down again. "He put the fire out. I wasn't making much head-way with it."

"You shouldn't have had to try at all," she answered indig-nantly. "Those frightful—"

"Now, now," Uncle Ben said. "No more inquests. We've had enough already, God knows." He took the stopper out of the decanter. "I think your young man has just arrived."

"Peter?"

"Wasn't that his car in the drive?"

"I didn't see it."

"You wouldn't. From here. The noise, I mean."

"I didn't recognise it. The traffic outside drowns everything."

"Not quite." Uncle Ben's voice was reduced to a faint whisper. "I was right. Here he comes."

Peter appeared on the walk beside the bougainvillaeas.

"I saw the lights and thought you might be here," he said, explaining his arrival. "Good evening, sir. I hope I'm not late. Evening, Alison."

"Good evening," she answered politely. Peter in a neat suit with his hair well brushed and a recent shave looked wonder-ful. She was glad she was wearing a dress she had got specially for tropical evenings, a very plain, well-cut sleeveless cream muslin with a shining gold sequin pattern in a narrow strip at the neck and sprinkling down to a point in front. Above it her auburn hair glowed richly.

Uncle Ben poured sherry, Peter handed glasses. Conversation

was desultory, with long pauses. But whatever tension there had been between the three of them was dissipated altogether by the time Jim came out to announce that dinner was served.

The Mancinis were standing in the dining room waiting to receive these honoured, these dangerous, these detestable guests. They bowed deeply. Mrs Mancini retreated to her own table, Luigi offered the menu to Alison while Jim handed another to Mr Wilberforce, who glanced at it and passed it on to Peter. After this Mr Mancini joined his wife.

The dinner was very good. Prompted by Jim the party chose as they were meant to do and Therese had excelled herself. Both Peter and Alison realised that they had eaten nothing since breakfast. Uncle Ben watched them with amusement, enjoying his own much smaller helpings.

About halfway through the meal the three Americans walked in. They stood still in amazement at sight of the quiet candle-lit well-dressed trio eating away contentedly while the men told anecdotes from their professional lives and the girl listened, encouraged them and occasionally made them laugh with some well-timed comment.

"Gee!" whispered Sam. "British phlegm in action again and how! We sure have seen a mouthful!"

Ray silenced him with a gesture and led the way forward.

"Hi, folks," he said cheerfully as he passed the diners. To which greeting Peter answered "Hi!" Alison said, "Hullo!" and Mr Wilberforce raised a limp hand.

Presently four Fernandans came in and took seats at a table on the opposite side of the room to the white strangers. The murmur of conversation grew. Jim was delighted. A boy appeared in a white jacket too large for him to help with the added numbers.

The Mancinis finished their meal and left. Luigi was still stunned by the events of the morning. Maria, less affected and always more practical, simply moaned about the loss of Paula at a time when the hotel was likely to have a boost from the publicity it was attracting.

"Two more couples arrive tomorrow, you say?" she asked, dropping the subject of Paula's general excellence, which raised no answering enthusiasm in her husband.

Mr Mancini nodded.

"And six next week," he said. "But it will not last and then we shall be worse off than ever. Besides, if too many come, Mr Wilberforce may leave and without our zombie who will want to stay here?"

"Be careful how you speak," Maria said, crossing herself and looking about her fearfully. "We know it is a superstition but the old man is dangerous. That is obvious."

"The insurance is a washout," grumbled Mancini. "All cancelled, as I told you before. Well, he is alive. That is natural."

"Also Silver is in gaol and likely to stay there," said his wife. "So there is no one to give a certificate of accident."

"Forget it!" shouted Luigi in a sudden fury. "Forget it was ever suggested!"

"You will not forget it when that superintendent hears you shouting," she answered. "He is to be here at nine to take coffee with those British."

"And you never tell me," Mr Mancini said in a hopeless voice. "If he *heard*!"

"If he heard he would be here now," she answered. "So shut up and be thankful we have our zombie still."

She crossed herself again, just in case, kicked off her pinching, high heeled shoes, then put her feet up on another chair and closed her eyes. Luigi turned up their transistor radio and did likewise.

Coffee was brought to Mr Wilberforce's room as soon as Graham arrived. He had no news for them about Gary Wilkins. The two passenger liners had been searched at their berths and warned to keep a watch for stowaways. The smaller cargo ships of all kinds had been searched and then told to anchor out in the harbour for that night and return to their berths in the morning.

"And the fishing boats?" asked Uncle Ben.

Graham shrugged.

"If he had money—" he said and left it at that.

"Even if he had money," Peter suggested, "where would they land him? They come back here, surely?"

"There are those small islands we call cays," Graham said. "If he had friends—"

Again he left his sentence unfinished. The whole subject of Gary Wilkins seemed to have lost interest for him.

After a short silence he said to Uncle Ben, "When I told you I had news for you I did not mean this bad nephew. It was about Stein, you know."

"Yes?"

"That Dr Stone is in Argentina with others of his family. It is beyond doubt he brought Manfred here to rob you, Colonel Wilberforce, and perhaps to kill you. He deliberately misled Dr Grigg as to your heart condition. This was to frighten you and to make you more agreeable to give your estate to a man you were to suppose was your nephew."

"I thought that was about the size of it," Uncle Ben said, cheerfully. "Bad luck for the Nazi thugs my real nephew turned up, equally murderous and a definite competitor."

"That is so," said Graham, smiling broadly. "I must make apology for suspecting you, Colonel. But in murder one must suspect everyone."

"Quite right. Even the slightly inadequate Dr Grigg, I imagine?"

"Why, yes. But Dr Grigg is having a normal holiday, quite open, quite innocent. He returns to Great Britain shortly."

"What about those two New Yorkers who also left here the morning you found Stein? Don't tell me you didn't check them, too."

Graham laughed heartily. Heartlessly, too, Alison thought.

"Yes, man, we checked! Did we check? They was out of their minds, so angry. Their ambassador had to know, they must have compensation for missing the plane. Routine check, you know. Nothing wrong."

Again there was silence. It was time for Graham to take his leave or else disclose what he had really come for. But he continued to sip coffee, sitting squarely on one of Uncle Ben's two upright chairs.

At last Peter guessed the reason. Stretching out a hand to Alison he said to her, "If Mr Wilberforce will excuse us, I think we might take a turn in the garden, don't you?"

As he held the door of the room open for the girl to pass Peter heard the old man whisper, "Penny dropped at last! Now, Graham, about Security—"

Later still that evening the three Americans arrived at Uncle Ben's door. Doggedly pursuing their purpose on San Fernando they had come to bargain with the live owner of Barrack Hill.

It was not difficult. Colonel Wilberforce, as Ray insisted upon addressing him, was perfectly willing to sell them the coffee estate, provided he kept the Barrack Hill Hotel, where he had, he told them, over the years established a regular set of guests for the hot summer months among the better-off professional class in Princeton.

"Over the years?" Chester Bilton asked, astonished. "I thought you'd not been in this place above a twelvemonth."

"Here at Gardenia Lodge, yes, that's perfectly true. But I acquired the estate while I was still working on the—er—the mainland of South America. I used to stay at Barrack Hill for a few weeks from time to time."

Ray nodded thoughtfully.

"That nephew of yours was sure off the beat," he said. "However, you've decided to let us have the estate, I gather."

"The estate, yes," said Uncle Ben, smoothly. "But for a concession to work the minerals you appear to have found there I'm afraid you'll have to apply to the government of San Fernando. They may consent or they may not. I can't tell you. They might even decide to requisition the whole thing from me, giving me rather poor compensation for the compulsory purchase and then developing the bauxite themselves.

They have the means to do so, as you may have noticed on your way in from the airport."

"Holy smoke!" exclaimed Sam. "And this calls itself a modern civilised independent state!"

"Independent indeed," answered Mr Wilberforce. "But quite ready to imitate the behaviour now unfortunately common in the former colonial power."

The three conferred by looks, nods and gestures, much to Mr Wilberforce's amusement. He suggested they might like to think things over together, but Ray, with the evident approval of his partners, shook his head.

"We'd like to deal primarily with you for the estate, Colonel," he said. "We may have means to get past those other problems you mention. Can we hear your figure?"

A short period of hard bargaining followed. For all his feeble appearance and faint voice Uncle Ben held his own without difficulty. The general lines of an agreement were written down and initialled by all present.

"I understand your lawyer in this place is—well, no longer available," Ray said, delicately.

"Poor Henry!" The old man sighed. "But young Grant is still here and as he represents the firm in London my family have dealt with for three generations at least, I think we can use him with every confidence, as they say."

Sam volunteered to go and find him, Chester went with him. They found him at the swimming pool with Alison in his arms, exchanging further details of their experiences of the last twenty-four hours in the intervals of long, satisfactory silences. So Peter was again interrupted in his intended proposal. It had seemed somehow pompous and irrelevant during this happy interval but the future must be planned, though it was perfectly clear that they both meant to spend it together.

In the short interval of time before his partners came back with Peter, Ray was shown a package by Mr Wilberforce which the latter took from his jacket pocket.

"May interest you," the old man said. "You *are* CIA, aren't you? I collected these privately over the last four years. My lot didn't want to meddle. Not through me, anyway. But I was interested."

"What are they?" Ray asked. He had expected his cover to be blown, but not quite in this way. Irregular—not quite—could be dangerous—

"Subversive stuff. Revolutionary. You come across all sorts, don't you? Manfred Stein ought to have known that. Amateur, I'm afraid, but nasty as they come. Well, take it or leave it."

He prepared to put away the package but Ray held out his hand for it.

"I take it you're selling this?" he said. "How much?"

"Certainly not, my dear chap." Colonel Wilberforce was affronted. "I told you this is the result of private investigations. Nothing to do with my boss or our interests, except indirectly. Besides, I wasn't the only pebble on those beaches. I acquired this stuff privately and I offer it to you for free." He paused, smiling. "On completion of the deal for the Barrack Hill site."

Ray took the package gingerly as if he feared it might blow up in his hands. He looked at some of the contents, his surprise and admiration growing.

"You can't simply have *asked* for this," he said, slowly. "Not without *something* given in exchange. Your people—"

"Didn't advance a penny for it. I got it privately. How many times must I insist upon that?"

"OK, OK," Ray answered. He handed back the package, which Mr Wilberforce now put into a drawer in his desk and turned the key on it. A moment later Ray's friends reappeared with Peter.

Alone in his own room that night Ray considered the contents of the package he had leafed through so rapidly. Dossiers, police case notes, photography, diaries, messages on rough paper—the lot. In bribes, in outright payments, in expenses, the old boy must have spent a fortune. For what? With what?

As a reward to the US for letting his crook brother settle in their territory, keeping him away from Britain? With part of the haul that the crook brother had stashed away in various foreign banks? Or was it his personal share in the haul?

All things were possible and he could never ask these questions, here or at home. So he would never know. Besides, provided the coffee plantation deal went through and he actually got the package it would be another small feather in his own cap. Or would it?

CHAPTER SEVENTEEN

Peter found his opportunity the following day. At breakfast, for which meal Peter arrived early to join Alison, the quiet Fernandan lady came to their table to explain that she found the present notoriety of Gardenia Lodge distasteful. She was going to her home near Freeman's Bay on the opposite shores of the island. She would be very pleased to drive them there, show them the country on the way, put them down on the beach or else the bank of a river where they could take a raft. After that she would like to invite them to a meal at her house and then show them where they could find a car to return them to Princeton.

They were only too pleased to accept this very generous offer. Peter had already managed to secure seats for them on a plane for England the next day, leaving in the afternoon and arriving at Heathrow early the following morning. Uncle Ben did not need them, probably would prefer to rest quietly alone. The sale of the estate was held up temporarily while Chester and Sam went over it in detail, comparing maps and plans and figures with their own findings. There would be a short business meeting of all parties the next morning, when such documents as could by then be drawn up would be exchanged.

The drive across the island was delightful and an interesting contrast with the mountain trip, for they went first through the old Spanish town of Santa Maria, the first capital, much diminished in extent, shorn of all authority, but not of a few central glories of architecture, far superior to anything now standing in prosperous, commercial Princeton.

Beyond Santa Maria they drove up a lush valley, with banana plantations and sugar cane and citrus fruits and many spice trees, nutmeg and achene in abundance. Also groves of cocoa trees, the large pods, many coloured from yellow to purple, hanging from the branches or fallen to the ground. Parrots flew from tree to tree across the road, small children led goats or flocks of shorn creatures with dark flapping ears that were the local sheep.

Presently the road came out beside a slow-running muddy river and this they followed for many miles, round bends and along straight reaches overhung by trees until the banks rose on either side and they left it to turn into another valley and so on towards the sea.

Their kind hostess followed exactly the programme she had laid before them at the breakfast table. They all spent an hour on the beach, playing in the Atlantic rollers and wishing they had brought surf boards with them. Afterwards they drove out again towards the river which, without seeming to increase its pace, wound back and forth between marshy flats to find its way into the ocean.

"You must have only a short rafting trip," they were told. "It will soon be too hot for it. The man will bring you to the last stage and I will be there to meet you."

So Peter's proposal, so much on his mind since the day before, finally found expression in the fewest words possible as he sat beside Alison on the broad raft looking at the shining ebony back and arms of the man with the pole standing just in front of them.

Peter's arm was round Alison, her head rested comfortably on his shoulder.

"This is the first time I've really had you to myself since I got here," he said. "Without interruptions, I mean."

"M—m," she agreed lazily and could not help adding, to encourage him. "But you really came to see Uncle Ben, didn't you?"

"No," he snapped. They had turned a bend in the river, the distant sea came into view, a wharf appeared at the end of the reach, the figure of their hostess standing there with binoculars trained, at present, on the beach beyond.

Time was again closing in on him, moreover his love's head was acting as a kind of poultice to his left collarbone and his arm, when he moved it, stuck to her dress.

"No," he repeated, sitting up away from her but steadying her with his hand. "I came to see *you*, my darling. To ask you to marry me. You will, won't you?"

"Of course I will, darling liar," Alison said calmly. "What else, d'you suppose?"

She leaned across to kiss him very slowly, very tenderly, so that Peter responded with such thankful fervour that the raft had rocked gently to a standstill before either of them noticed that they had arrived at the landing-stage. Their quiet hostess was still tactfully gazing out to sea through her binoculars.

Superintendent Graham called on Mr Wilberforce that morning before he left his room. There was news of Gary Wilkins at last.

"My men have found him near the mouth of the harbour," he said. "Quite dead, of course. On the beach just outside the point. Drowned. The pilot boat informed us when they saw the body."

"What was he doing out there?" Uncle Ben asked, but without much interest.

"I think I shall not have clear detail in this case," Graham answered stiffly. "Exhausted when swimming, the inquest will no doubt bring in. His embassy will not complain, you know."

"All the same you must have a bit more information or you would not look so exactly like a cat after cream now," Mr Wilberforce insisted.

"The news comes not directly but by Vincent from the waterside. I get Inspector Vincent into my branch now. Very promising—very—very—keen."

"Thorough," Uncle Ben suggested.

"That is exact. Thorough. By talk, here and there, Vincent finds one too many for the crew of a certain boat. He watches. Correct number go on board. He still watches. They take up man out of the water after they leave pier. He has waited, swimming around. The boat is for St Thomas. It is for money. He has paid money."

"In advance? Incredible!"

"As you say. Vincent reports. We wait. These trading boats have radio, you know. So I wait. When the boat is well outside the harbour I send radio police message. Search will be made of all ships in territorial waters for escaped murderer. I give description. If found all on board will be arrested as accomplices."

"And that worked?"

"As you say, man. They just put him overboard again. It was a bit too far for him. He drowned."

"He had bad luck," said Mr Wilberforce, "but he didn't deserve any better. He was a vicious, useless character and as greedy as they come. Always after something for nothing. In the end he *got* nothing, not even his life."

Superintendent Graham opened his mouth to ask one more question, but thought better of it. He would get no answer from the old man but he would dearly like to know why Wilkins had come at all to San Fernando. Three times altogether, prospecting in the coffee plantation, making up to Paula, away from Gardenia Lodge, of course, laying some sort of careful plot that had, apparently, gone wrong at every stage. A twisted plot and he felt sure the ends had never been tied. Nor would they be now. You could go just so far with Colonel Wilberforce and no further. He had gone that far: he had reached that dead end.

After his conversation with Graham was over the old man went out to the verandah. He sat there until lunch time, reading the newspaper. Afterwards he retired to his room to sleep. He got up again at the usual time; Jim brought him his tea with some small freshly baked cakes, neatly iced by Therese. He was tasting one of these when the Americans drove up to the office.

At once he put the unfinished bun on his plate and shambled along the outside path to the drive. The three were loading a pile of suitcases into the boot of their car, but stopped when they saw him. Ray came forward.

"We were going to look for you," he began rather lamely.

"Going away?" Uncle Ben asked, waving a long thin hand at their pile of luggage.

"Only up to Four Paths," Ray said in a lowered voice. "Think a change advisable. We don't want to be mixed into your drama and—"

"The drama is over," Mr Wilberforce said, quietly. "My nephew's body was found just round the point of the harbour early this morning. He had been swimming and did not quite make the beach. The inquest was to be early this afternoon. Death by drowning, I believe."

"I'm—sorry," Ray said, looking for a better word but not finding it.

"I'm not," said Uncle Ben. "But I don't blame you for moving. You want to see me, I suppose?"

He turned as if sure of the answer and walked the few steps up the corridor to his room. The others, beckoned by Ray, followed.

They were all a little awkward, Mr Wilberforce saw, a bit embarrassed, not quite the set of brisk business men with whom he had drawn up a provisional agreement for the sale of his estate.

"The fact is," Sam began and stopped, looking at his companions for support.

"We've been over that patch of ground with a fine comb," Chester stated. "It's not—well, it's not just what we were led to expect."

"By my nephew," Uncle Ben added. "Not—I repeat *not*— by me."

"Sure, sure," the two agreed hastily. Ray said nothing.

"So—" Mr Wilberforce encouraged them gently.

"So as Sam isn't happy about the yield of bauxite we're likely to get we think the price—" Chester tailed off before the steady gleam in the old man's eyes. Ray still said nothing.

The silence continued until Mr Wilberforce, rousing himself with an apparent effort, said in a near whisper, "Now that the late Gary Wilkins has demonstrated to you very fully his remarkably criminal character you should not be so surprised to find he has misled you over the mineral worth of my coffee estate. I hope I have made plain that I personally have never tried to discover it, have no knowledge of such things and have simply accepted your own figures and estimates. But—" he quelled an interruption from Sam with one upraised finger, "but I must tell you that I have been surprised, not so much by your reliance on that plausible rogue, my nephew, as by the fact that the government here have been so little interested in your project. You have, I take it, approached them for planning permission?"

"They said they saw no undue difficulty in granting it," Chester agreed, sulkily.

"Quite so. I have never been approached by them myself with a view to development. I warned you to consider this angle. You missed the implication, it seems."

"Then it will be no surprise to you if we withdraw our offer," said Sam, defiantly. "With appropriate compensation, though the full contract was not finally drawn up."

With his eyes now turned on Ray Leadbetter, Mr Wilberforce said quietly, "It would surprise me very much indeed."

"The deal will go through," said Ray. And when the other two half rose in their chairs, red-faced and indignant, he went on, "D'you mind, fellers? I know how I can fix it. No hard feelings, eh, Colonel?"

The two younger men blinked, exchanged looks and retreated. When they had gone Ray said, "A neat piece of blackmail. Colonel Wilberforce," and leaned back in his chair.

The old man was unmoved. He said, "Not at all, Leadbetter. I offered you, as a present, some documents you found interesting. In exchange your group were to buy my coffee estate which you appeared to find of considerable worth. I employed no experts, no valuers. You had two experts to advise you. It is not my fault if you brought one very young man and one insufficiently experienced. Nor that you seem all to have been deceived by a practised crook. I was not deceived. However, to keep your associates happy and prevent them looking for your ulterior motives I will make a few concessions. Mr Grant has already agreed to make out a legal form of the contract this evening when he comes in from his outing with my niece and will bring it here for signing before witnesses tomorrow morning."

He unfolded the draft agreement, turning it towards Ray, inviting him to draw up his chair and begin discussion of detail.

Ray, who had now been struck by the same thought that had occurred to Superintendent Graham, said, "Gary must have known all along the estate didn't hold much bauxite."

"Perhaps. I have no idea. That wouldn't stop him."

"But he wanted it for himself. The whole lot, everything you had. What was he really looking for, Colonel?"

Uncle Ben's face did not change. He merely lifted his shoulders a little.

"He was not in my confidence," he said. "And now—"

The shoulders came down, settled firmly. A coffin lid, Ray thought, in place and nailed up tight.

The taxi dropped Peter at the Marshalls' and took Alison back to Gardenia Lodge. It was not very late and the light was still on in Uncle Ben's room so she stepped across to the verandah and knocked at his door.

"Are you busy?" she asked as she went in.

He was sitting at his desk with a pile of loose papers before him. His voice, as he had called 'Come in', had been strong and calm as was the face he turned to her over his shoulder.

"I just wanted to tell you Peter and I are engaged," she said. "I hope you approve."

He got up at once, took her hands in his and kissed her on both cheeks. In her new total happiness she clung to him laughing, but with tears in her eyes. This poor old uncle, so broken-down, so ill and yet so terrifying.

"You did that just as you used to," she stammered, adding, "when I was little. Too long ago. Why did you never come home?"

It had all flowed out without thought for him, only for her own life deprived of his affection, now bestowed on her again.

"I'm sorry," she said, seeing his face change. "I don't know what I'm saying. I'm so happy."

"Which is as it should be," he answered. "Sit down."

"No. It's getting late and you're busy. I'll see you in the morning. We don't have to start for the airport till lunch time. Night flight. Via Bermuda."

He moved his papers together at one side of the desk, disclosing as he did so an oval miniature in a neat leather case with a supporting leg like a picture frame.

Alison saw it, saw that it was a small painting of a dark woman with large eyes and smiling lips, with abundant curls through which a single strand of pearls wandered, wearing a white dress frilled at the high neck.

"Who's that?" she asked, stretching a hand to it. "May I?"

As he did not answer she picked it up. The face was beautiful and strange.

"An ancestor?" she asked gaily. "Regency, isn't she? Your side, of course. No Scot."

"Certainly not. She isn't an ancestor. She isn't anyone I ever met. She just reminds me of someone—someone I was fond of when I was—young—a boy."

"You mean you picked this up and kept it because she reminded you of someone?"

"Yes, my dear. Exactly that."

"She's beautiful. Do you always have her on your desk? I haven't seen her before."

He laughed softly.

"There has not been much opportunity, has there?"

There had not, indeed. Obviously he took the miniature about with him in its little leather case. Poor old Uncle Ben! Who would have guessed he had a buried romance? Of course he must have been quite attractive, even good looking when he was young. Perhaps they'd know at home—

She said goodnight, kissed him again without allowing him to get up and said over his shoulder, "I do think she's lovely. Will you leave her to me in your will?"

She felt him stiffen, but he said lightly, matching her own gay tones, "Certainly not. I shall have her buried with me in my own grave."

She patted his shoulder and went away to her bed. When she had gone Uncle Ben sat for some time looking at his miniature, before moving it to one side and drawing back the pile of papers, bills, letters and other innocuous matters that had suffered the confusion of police notice during his disappearance.

For much of the next morning Peter was shut up with Mr Wilberforce and Ray Leadbetter who had come to complete the sale of the coffee estate. Various complicated legal procedures had been by-passed, Peter found, by a combined effort of the British High Commissioner and the United States Embassy, with the approval or at any rate the permission of the San Fernandan government. At the end of it all a car arrived with various high ranking officials to act as witnesses of the signatures of the principals. This done Ray went off with the representative of his own government while the rest, British and Fernandan, removed to the verandah where Mr Wilberforce ordered cooling drinks for all.

The Marshalls had come with the High Commissioner's representative. Mrs Marshall, leaving the men to their drinks, found Alison in her room, packing.

"I just came along to congratulate you," she said. "Peter told us last night. I may say it was not altogether a surprise to us."

"Nor me," said Alison, smiling happily. "We've known each other in London for ages," she added, to explain this oversimplification.

Peter went away with the Marshalls to fetch his luggage in a taxi that would pick up Alison on the way to the airport. They wanted to avoid a ceremonial lunch. Besides, it was Uncle Ben's day to visit the hospital and after all the excitement since his last attendance there they thought he should be relieved of their presence in good time.

While Peter took a few last instructions from the old man in his role of family solicitor, Alison slipped round to the kitchen to find Therese, who shed a few tears of thankfulness mixed with regret and clasped both the girl's hands in a painfully strong grip.

"Therese," Alison said, to take the other's mind off the parting, "I can't thank you enough for all the wonderful food you've cooked for me. I think Uncle Ben is very lucky to have you."

"He eats nothing, Missy Maclean. A sparrow."

"He's very old," the girl said, "and ill and perhaps sad— lonely."

She had remembered the miniature. Therese's eyes brightened.

"You see that picture?" she said, lowering her voice. "That lady? Is back from yesterday. I know it well. I wonder, too."

Alison nodded.

Therese went on, "He let me—only me—clean his room. Lizzie take coffee for breakfast. Only Therese sweeps and dust."

"Who is she?"

"He never say. But I think not from England. Jim laugh, but I say she like lady where I born. That's Guadalupe, missy. Creole lady—we say. Mas'r Wilb go all about these islands. Maybe meet—maybe she die—"

Alison laughed gently.

"You're just as romantic as I am," she said, pressing the big hands again.

Outside Peter was calling for her.

"You not keep him waiting," Therese said, giving her a little push. "Mans always impatient. I know."

She followed the girl to the door, smiling broadly now at their joint absurdity.

Uncle Ben was affable, affectionate. Alison kissed him good-bye with genuine feeling. She did not urge him to come to England for her wedding because she knew it would be impossible. But she promised to write, hoping her resolve would not weaken.

The Mancinis stood on the little verandah, watching. Alison said goodbye to them politely from a little distance, bowing, avoiding handshakes.

Jim opened the taxi door for her and looking into his grave, contained face and eyes saddened by her going she was suddenly overcome with warm gratitude and admiration for his single-minded devotion to her uncle and herself. She put an arm round his neck as he bowed over the door and kissed his cheek.

"We can never thank you enough, Jim," she said, ducking away on to the seat of the taxi.

"She's right, Jim," Peter said, gripping the waiter's hand as he followed.

Jim went back to Therese and she slipped her arm through his.

"You shameless man!" she told him. "You kiss white women now, you black trash!"

"Missy Wilb kiss me," Jim answered dreamily, then catching his wife's indulgent eye he burst into a great laugh and pulled her round into his arms.

Lunch at the Princeton airport was ample but unappetising. After it Alison and Peter looked for paperbacks or periodicals to occupy them on the flight until nightfall and the dimming of lights later on in the cabin.

They were in the air again after a brief stop at Bermuda when Alison tugged at Peter's sleeve.

"Look!" she said. "D'you see what I see?"

It was a photograph of a miniature of a woman with a string of pearls in her dark hair and a white dress, frilled at the neck.

"What is it?" he said.

"It's the living image of Uncle Ben's miniature. Didn't you see it on his desk?"

"No."

"Then he must have put it away while you and Ray were in his room. I'm not surprised."

"Why?"

"Read the article."

Art thefts were on the increase, the article explained. Thefts and the manufacture of fakes. Every year for a long time now, but on an increasing scale, private and public collections had been attacked and despoiled. There was an underground market for these things. Many were too well-known to reappear. They went into the possession of cranks who were willing to pay vast sums simply to enjoy personally an objet d'art they could never display to others. For instance the two articles illustrated, a unique gold snuff box stolen—

"The miniature!" Alison interrupted. "Look—"

And a miniature of Josephine, first wife of Napoleon Buona-parte, stolen over twenty years ago from—

"By my Uncle George, I don't mind betting," said Alison. "And now in the private—the very private—collection of my Uncle Ben—the old fox. As calm—as a mill pond—"

"And as weedy."

"Funny, ha-ha. He didn't even tell a lie. He said it reminded him of someone he once knew. And I was sold on it being a tragical romance!"

Peter was thoughtful.

"So Gary Wilkins was right. There *was* treasure. He wasn't being ridiculously mad as well as viciously bad."

"But he didn't know what to look for. Even if his father ever told him, which I doubt."

After a time Peter said, "What can we do?"

"Nothing," Alison answered firmly. "We can't *prove* anything, can we? There may have been umpteen reproductions."

"Quite. We aren't even sure *you* aren't making a mistake."

"Oh no." She was certain in her own mind. "Therese even said she was a creole lady. She's partly French herself, Therese. Naughty old Uncle Ben. I don't think I really like him. Do you?"

"A disturbing character," said Peter, gruffly.

"Oh darling, how pompous! Don't turn into the complete lawyer *yet*."

She settled down with her head against his arm, tipping back her chair as the stewardess dimmed the lights. Peter gave a sigh of content. He was half asleep already. But as the stewardess passed him he handed her the magazine and told her to put it in the dustbin. Just as well for Alison to forget it, he decided. Or at least have nothing to show to her friends.

In San Fernando Mr Wilberforce visited the hospital and saw Dr Faulkner. The latter was delighted to hear a straightforward, concise account of the old man's adventures of the last week, in place of the scrappy, confused and sensational newspaper paragraphs.

He made a careful examination. Colonel Wilberforce was no better and no worse for it all, he decided. He put the patient back on the pills Dr Grigg had given him originally, advised a slight change of diet and told him a fortnightly visit would probably be sufficient in the foreseeable future. The old man was quite satisfied with these small changes in his regime.

Late that evening he called Jim to go with him to the swimming pool. On the way back after his bathe he stopped and said, "Jim, I think the Mancinis will soon give up this place. When the rush of sightseers is over it will be even more unpopular than before, I think."

"I think so, too," Jim agreed.

"So I will go to live at Barrack Hill, Jim, and I want you and Therese to come and live with me there. Not before Mancini goes. But when he decides to do that. Will you come?"

"Whenever you say, Mas'r Wilb."

They walked on till they reached the drive. Mr Wilberforce stopped again.

"There's one thing more, Jim," he said. "I have not forgotten you in my will. But it is something more. I have a small picture I keep near me. Therese knows. She likes it. I see her look at it when she dusts my room."

Jim nodded, gravely.

"When I die, Jim, I want you to put that little picture in my coffin with me." He paused, looking up at the bright stars, speaking more to them than to the companion at his side. "It has no negotiable value now and I want it to go when I go. Because it reminds me of someone I loved very much as a boy and who did me a great and lasting wrong. He was my brother, Jim, my elder brother. He was the hero of my childhood, he never quite lost that position." His voice sank to an inaudible whisper. "He gave me the picture, which he had taken from a dealer who had himself stolen it. A priceless and useless gift. Like himself. Priceless and useless, dangerous and death-dealing."

Poor old Wilb, Jim thought, watching him move slowly towards the verandah. Poor old Wilb, doesn't know what he's saying, he told himself, propping up the rubber mattress outside the kitchen door.

If you have enjoyed this book, you might wish to join the Walker British Mystery Society.

For information, please send a postcard or letter to:

Paperback Mystery Editor

Walker & Company
720 Fifth Avenue
New York, NY 10019